it had been
Planned been
and there were
guides

PRAISE FOR *IT HAD BEEN PLANNED AND THERE WERE GUIDES*

"This book has heart and heft and heat and equal doses of wonder and quirk to keep us on our toes, not knowing what might be waiting for us, not just on the next page but inside the next sentence. Richardson's tongue is an organ of the eye. Her prose sings cleanly, her ear hears with its hand not just cupped around it but it reaches out to pull us in and hold us all a little closer."

—Peter Markus, author of *The Fish and the Not Fish, We Make Mud*, and *The Singing Fish*

"You know how you keep that piece of paper and pen next to the bed to capture those brilliantly enriched osmotic *mots justes* emanating from the edge of the edge of waking sleep? And you know how the vivid quarry eludes you; how you're left with the snare of scribbles, memories of memory, in the morning light? The stories in Jessica Lee Richardson's teeming *It Had Been Planned and There Were Guides* are goddamned Google maps of those saturated hypnopompic, hypnagogic states, rendered with such exacting detail and pristine clarity that you can do nothing more than conclude the murky margins of the world have been turned inside out and the meanest meanings ever meant are sunbathing there, plain as day."

—Michael Martone, author of *Michael Martone* and *Four for a Quarter*

"'Then a surprising thing happened, which is that we didn't die.' Jessica Lee Richardson's brief, jagged, lit-up stories present a world of precarity in which the precincts of the sentence propel the protagonists towards and away from peril with the capriciousness of wanton gods: 'I dropped through the trap door at the bottom of the bottom and came out on top.' In this world of prodigious and acute risk, in which every angel is drug tested and Baby Girl Bristol reads the writing on the wall, radiant hyperfluency is both a necessary skill and an interface through which all the toxic mediumicity of our present moment can flood. 'I looked in the mirror and it was like I could see the halo. Now I have Beyoncé in my head. Google.' Amen."

—Joyelle McSweeney, author of *Salamandrine: 8 Gothics* and *Dead Youth, or, The Leaks*

it had been planned and there were guides

stories

jessica lee richardson

FC2

TUSCALOOSA

FC2 is an imprint of The University of Alabama Press

Inquiries about reproducing material from this work should be addressed to the University of Alabama Press

Book Design: Publications Unit, Department of English, Illinois State University; Codirectors: Steve Halle and Jane L. Carman; Assistant Director: Danielle Duvick; Production Assistant: Elora Karim
Cover Art: Sebastián Patané Masuelli
Cover Design: Lou Robinson
Typeface: Warnock Pro
⊗
The paper on which this book is printed meets the minimum requirements of American National Standard for Information Sciences—Permanence of Paper for Printed Library Materials, ANSI Z39.48–1984

Library of Congress Cataloging-in-Publication Data

Richardson, Jessica Lee, 1978-
[Short stories. Selections]
It had been planned and there were guides : stories / Jessica Lee Richardson.
pages cm
ISBN 978-1-57366-052-5 (pbk. : alk. paper) -- ISBN 978-1-57366-856-9 (ebook)
I. Title.
PS3618.I34465A6 2015
813'.6--dc23
2015012189

for the J's

table of contents

it had been
planned
and there were
guides

descent

call me silk

They come in a truck. They are a man and a woman, but really they are just the man. I don't wish to describe him. The truck has a commercial bed, closed white box, and it's from within it that the couple do all of their smiling and offering of warm drinks. I'll describe the woman. She has a wonderful smile. That's not a specific description is it? She has shoulder length brown hair, curly. Her mouth wags out wide and shoots joy teeth into crow's feet like blankets. How's that? She nods a lot, reassuringly, with the smile. The man, here I am doing it, it's hard not to picture him. I don't want to give you this problem. But have you ever seen the drawings of the strange man that thousands of people all claim to have dreamed? It's scary to look at him because he has a face that lives at the edges of dream. Which is to say that while all of the components of his face are familiar, the arrangement is not. The guy in the truck is like that. Except much cozier looking than the man thousands of people have dreamed.

I don't know the names of the familiar man and woman. You'd think I'd have gotten them. I was too busy feeling safe in the back of a truck, with this couple that looked like aging parents, that by the looks of it have an infant grandchild somewhere with toes to tickle. I guess I still wanted parents. Or to be tickled.

The man was bald and a nodder too, though his smile was thinner than the woman's. I felt lighthearted in their presence. Except that's not right because it's just a term. My heart literally felt light, airy, but the impression of this full floating heart was dead serious and my limbs grew heavy as magnets while my lungs soared. It was clear this couple was up to something. They offered me tea just because I peeked into their truck. They were so constant with the smiling.

In my naïveté I thought it was Christianity they were up to. One of the weirder kinds, maybe, the rapturous. So I was naturally hesitant about the free tea. The air feeling I had propelled me into the truck, though, and they offered me a cushion. They had cushions lying around. The kind tied to the backs of kitchen chairs, except no kitchen chairs. Just the nod-smiling and a nearly imperceptible encroaching. They came closer and closer to me, physically, as we talked. They never mentioned anything religious, but everything about them continued to imply it. I started trying to back away and that's when I had no choice about the tea despite my right hand raised in protest. I was suddenly sipping it because the man was suddenly holding my head back and pressing the mug into my mouth. I didn't spit the tepid tea water in his face. He was breathing on my neck and his old man cheeks smelled like cheese. His pupils had taken on a much less paternal, much more concentrated gaze. My chest still felt like it had broken into a feathery dream, though. I was in some sort of chest-based heaven, so I began to feel like the tea was important, like these people maybe had something better than Christianity inside them. Like they knew something more than me, something that elevated the air around them, the people. I sipped.

I guess they probably did have something elevating and I guess it was some sort of drug. It did not resemble any drug experience I've ever known. I've taken some drugs, who hasn't? In this case "drug" is an oversimplification and maybe always is.

The man did not know more than me. I was not elevated, in fact, I went down when I swallowed, and when I did, I was in a swimming pool. The man was with me in the pool, in the exact same position as he was in the truck, pulling my head back, pressing into me. His dick was hard, I could feel it against me. It was smothering me, more so than a simple body could, this dick and man. I felt like my own bones were shrinking and squishing the rest of me into a space I didn't fit in. All of me raging against my frame. It tasted like chlorine, this death I was sure was upon me. Like cum with a hint of old man face.

Then it was over. I woke up beside where the truck had been and the truck was gone. Clearly the couple was gone too. I guess it could have been roofies. That's the logical explanation. I had been unconscious but had emerged with a sliver of swimming pool dreaming. I was shaken, but felt otherwise unchanged. I was wrong, though, about being unchanged.

It could have been coincidence, but coincidence has its limits. However strange coincidence can be, it isn't perfect. This is a story of perfection.

After I woke by the truck, I started taking risks. Not normal risks. Insane risks. I took my first one that same night. I'll tell you about it in a second. I want to explain that these risks I take don't ever kill me. I keep upping the danger levels, mainly because I can't help it, but partly to test that theory. I continually do not die. I'm sure I can die, like any living thing, but I seem unable to die while taking these risks. Another strange thing about the risks is that I always wind up in a swimming pool. There will not be a detectable swimming pool anywhere near the risk that's gotten inside me. That's how it is, by the way, the risk gets inside me. I don't know why I want to enact this frightful idea, I only feel that I'll die if I don't. But no matter how far from swimming pools the risk is, I wind up in one at the completion. Within mere hours, I'm always in a pool I did not seek out.

Explain this to me. Please.

The first one, okay, the first pool on that first night, I did seek out. I didn't make the connection. I just got the inclination that I must jump from the top of a house. I left the dirt by the side of the now non-existent truck and found the tallest house I could. I climbed it from the outside. I didn't want to break my legs, so when I saw the pool in the back yard beyond the turret, I aimed for it. The splash woke the family, but I was too busy enjoying the cold blue eternity-in-a-moment feeling. I didn't notice them staring. So I got fished out and had to explain. I really couldn't, either, I mostly just shivered and apologized dumbly, shaking my head.

I had a lot of explaining to do in those first months. Most people decided I was crazy and you probably will too. It's easy to call people like me crazy. Most people like easy. So I'll spare you detail and give you a montage. I exhausted building climbing and leaping pretty quickly and used all of my savings on extreme sports expeditions. I tried hang gliding, skydiving, base-jumping, many kinds of boarding—sand, snow, wave. You can imagine how weird it was to wind up in a pool on snowy mountain peaks, but I'm telling you, pools are everywhere. They snuck snaking around the globe at some point in architectural history. I grew restless with each sport, ridding myself of more and more gear, footholds be damned. I jumped face down, tried wing suits, graduated to paragliding. I chose the highest, rockiest descents I could find. You may have read profiles on me because I couldn't help but attract attention, maybe because I'm a girl, though I wasn't the only girl doing the adrenaline thing. Still, someone was always tattling about my lack of precaution to the publications that crop up around fear hunger.

As a side note, I once got involved with a group of extreme ironers. They climb high peaks with an ironing board and when they get to the top, iron a shirt. I don't count the hilltop ironing as a part of the set of absurd missions that overtook me after meeting the couple in the truck, but I laughed a lot that day. I wasn't beyond humor despite how seriously I seemed to take myself.

I also wasn't much interested in the communities that surround these "aggro" sports. But you have to wiggle into them at first to hop rides and get a feel for terrains. I soon ran out of money, but stopped in resort towns and bartended for more funds. Sometimes I sold pot. I refused offers to advertise because it seemed to sterilize an activity of its danger to have the Budweiser logo streaming across your kitewing.

I want to explain, it wasn't that I lost my fear. I've stood at the top of Angel Falls with nothing but a piece of ripstop polyester and some string between me and falling into water moving at 9.8 meters per second, barreling into the rock of its midsection with a force great enough to chop off my limbs, seeing only through the fish eye lens of vertigo a height so high it's a skewed painting screaming with wind. Yes, I was trembling from head to foot. Some of the guys I was with didn't tremble like that. There is a way to lose fear, and I believe I understand how it's done. But I didn't want to lose my fear. I wanted to shake like that. Inside of that shake, if I closed my eyes, was the air chest, was a dream I never wake up from. Not the dream of the man. The dream I made with the materials at hand, my life.

There comes a point where you can no longer top yourself, though. Beyond committing suicide, there is no higher place to go, no faster, no fewer safety nets. People try. They combine features of multiple sports, like those parkour guys with the spring shoes. But combinations are a recipe for restlessness. The peak has been reached and frustration is the only result thereafter. I've seen it. The dudes that go that route wind up dead, and not even a glorious death, because it happens during some boneheaded inferior thrill. I never had the option to go down that path. My motivations sprung up from within, unavoidable as sucking on oxygen, and they were always scarier and scarier. But they changed course suddenly, so I must have peaked at Meru.

I wasn't the first to jump the Himalayan peak, but record setting never had anything to do with it for me. The pool that ended that day was obviously in the hotel, as it was for many of my escapades, but I never meant to wind up in any of them beyond the first. After Meru I got off on the wrong floor and of course it was the pool and of course I wanted to avoid it, but was pulled to peer into the water like my eyes were suction cups. And I kid you not, a little spindly kid with a pointy face pushed me into the deep end in my clothes. The same thing happened that always happens. I can't get out. I am under and under until I am fished. Blanketed and having to nod a lot and apologize and swear I wasn't trying to commit suicide in your hotel. After that, I had a brief flirtation with entering war zones. Then my obsessions quickly switched to love.

There is a point in love where you can slip the silk, as I call it. You are holding onto the silk, and then you loosen your grip and fall backwards in the romantic equivalent of one of those startling dreams that wake you with a hypnic jerk and a tummy flip. Sure, people do this every day, but there are some deep descents.

First I met Bob. He was a free soloist. I was still tooling around in adventure sports because I didn't know yet that my body had chosen new hurdles for me and in between impulse was practice for impulse. We did Yosemite together once I got in shape enough. It bored me, to be honest. I'm not making light of how dangerous it is to climb straight rock walls thousands of feet with nothing but your fingers and toes and severe exhaustion. It just wasn't my thing. I was longing to go back to Somalia to munch on rooti and dance with the Sufi in between insurrections. But watching him and his sexy command of the uncommandable was irresistible and I slipped the silk. Literally, first, on a practice climb with ropes. I fell. He took the opportunity to fuck me while we dangled, laughing, in a part of the chimney crevasse obscured from tourist view. It was all very sweet. At first. It took me three more loves to figure out that I was into some extreme loving now, physical danger having nothing on emotional danger.

What I had to do next was subjugate myself, further and further into the great pearl of power hiding at the dead center of utter humiliation. Fun stuff.

Bob's distant, slow retreat was a bunny butt compared to what was to come later. It was the classic scenario. Young sexy alpha gets bored once he knows he's won female's affection. You've heard this one. Chances are you've lived it from one side or the other, at one strata or another. I started baking and sticking sweet notes in his backpack. He started going to bars more, staying out later, taking over an hour to cum on the rare occasions we had sex. Ouch. Oh, that first slip slices. I didn't see it coming. I still had pride. I didn't understand the sickness.

We're going down now, are you ready? Hold onto your rope.

Next I loved a Dick whose name wasn't Dick. He was just an intellectual. I'm sure not all intellectuals are like this, but this one had a squint of disdain like a spike in his eye. Pointed at me, usually, when I spoke. We met at a party. We stood by a window and smoked cigarettes while I chewed olives. I was interesting to him because of my unique set of experiences. He was interesting to me because of his darting sparkler brain. But I should have understood by the way he referenced philosophers after my every sentence, comparing my last jump to prescriptions made by a man made mad by a horse, that he was seeing through me. Or rather, I was a bit of data to add to a nest of connections he needed to constantly plug together to feel validated. The story is boring, it adds up to this: enough squints pile over squints and it begins to smart. A laser aimed at your identity like it's a mole. A banana slicer separating the mush of your most precious truths. A father insisting you are a child. I loved him anyway. I loved even the small nervous boy inside of him, demanding he try to win at everything, even a glance. He often disappeared for months at a time not calling. Finally he told me I have bad genes because my grandmother is crazy, which she isn't, and disappeared for good.

I found myself in a pool. I greeted the clear weight now, the under and press of blue and bleach.

The next guy beat me up. This story makes me sound so un-feminist. I didn't understand until this abuser that these relationships were products of my old risk curse, which I'd assumed I had broken. I should have. I'd zoom in on these men in a bar, or at a bookstore (because now I'm reading philosophers too of course, linguists), or at a camp and I'd tunnel into them. My feet would walk me to them before my brain could interrupt. My affections would gather and swell my organs and blood from throat to vagina, filled to secretion like an untied water balloon. Swish I'd go. I didn't not leave the guy who beat me because I'm a battered woman type. I didn't leave him because everything inside me insisted itself upon the situation, wanted to pierce the membrane of it to get at what was behind. But probably no battered woman is a type. Maybe they all have risk curses, I don't know. He finally left me because I laughed through the blood bubbling through my teeth. He couldn't ever hurt me enough. He never even had to bring flowers of apology, I'd burrow under his armpits fetal, concussed with love. I will say to the women who are not, like me, on a quest for the scariest situation they can find, that the guy who beats you is not necessarily a big violent bruiser cussing at flies. He's hiding in crowds of perfectly nice seeming people. He may even be small and quiet, as mine was. Scary hides inside not scary. I miss him.

Pool.

Something happens when the worst of the worst keep abandoning you. They are telling you—YOU are the worst of the worst, because even I, shitty as I am, can't bear YOU. They enjoy showing you the extent of your shittiness. But so do you. Or I, I should say I. I was enjoying the displays, a part of me was.

The first of my adventures had to do with inclines. The last of them had to do with declines. At the lowest place there is nothing to lose anymore. No accusation can swing by that hasn't already arrowed into your face. There's freedom in that. In freedom there's a way back up. Of course, I didn't know that yet, not fully. I was programmed somehow, perhaps by a cup of tea in a truck, to put myself on the line.

Each love was stronger in its envelopment. I'd buzz to the tips of my toes, drool with ecstasy for each successive bum with more intensity. I mean bum, literally. There was a sequence—addict, sociopath, suicidal. The latter was tough. I loved him with the feral warmth of a mother layered over with the clutch of lust. When he pilled himself into the great oblivion he blamed me in the note.

Pool.

Finally, I fell blisteringly in love with a homeless man. It wasn't until then that I began to see the wisdom in these impulses of mine. Yes, the heartbreak was greater and greater. I couldn't even walk sometimes for the heaviness of so much longing stuffed in, the place for it to go all gone. The deafening pain of the blunt scoop of desire's sweet spoon. Here, eat, it says. But at some point you realize like old Thyestes that it's you there in the bowl. The child of you. I shuffled. I didn't tie my shoes. That's how I met Jarred. He saw my untied shoes and thought I was homeless too. I was close. I was staying on my brother's couch in downtown LA. He was the only family member left who still put up with me. It was hard to hold a job with all that pulsing and searing. Jarred asked if I had a cigarette. Of course I did. No gambler is without her pack of smokes. When my eyes met his, the feather plummet, the cool blue of recognition, the edges of his red eyes where they joined the lashes and the way they wouldn't look. I was mad for him. I'd wandered into the tent village, I noticed, as I looked for a slab of concrete where I could pull his body down and suck on it. Tents, even better. I put a tit in his mouth and pulled him in. He didn't protest. It's the way of the homeless, broken and slow, taking whatever comes. We came. We came and came and we shook the tent. He smelled terrible, like gas doused in vinegar and sharpened. I invited him back to my brother's place for a shower. It was how I was kicked out of any semblance of normalcy. Even family doesn't take to a homeless guy frying eggs in their kitchen.

Was there a moment? When I asked myself how a middle class girl with a decent education who'd had write ups about her in magazines, who'd even on occasion dined in five star

restaurants sipping Amarone, tonguing a quail bone, sucking raspberries from the rim of a two hundred dollar glass of
champagne, had wound up not only living in a tent village, but
without even a tent? At the bottom of the homeless hierarchy,
because even the broken sift and sort each other? With a boyfriend, feet exploded from his shoes into puffed pink rhinos,
who left me to fend for myself amongst virulent desperation
while he searched for his next fix? I was not the only one down
there you know. Educated, comparatively moneyed, once filled
with the breath of promise. You'd be surprised. Most people
don't begin at the bottom, even if they're unfortunate enough
to be born poor or brown, or even both. Some do begin at
the bottom, though. If you think I've caught some vistas, their
vision would fricassee your tender retinas to shards. But of
course, yes, there was a moment. It was when I was chasing
Jarred through the village at night, his nearly incomprehen-
sible mumbles adding up to "leave me alone" that I realized.
Fuck. But there was something under the fuck, as there always
is. First, of course, the pain. I was in love, after all. It doesn't
matter if you've grown accustomed to the grip of that ice fist,
heartbreak is a blind boxer that can find every weak spot by
touch, punch into the end of each wiggling appendage. Sobbing, I chased him. He wasn't very fast on those busted feet,
but he was resolute. The sweetness I'd seen in his buried eyes
was just want in its tearful mask, and it had sealed over dry.
Gone dead. There was nothing else I could give him.

I knew the landscape well enough to wipe my snot and
turn away, finally, when Jarred crumpled toward another
woman with accidental dreadlocks and a pregnant belly. I
thought I'd trade sex for some heroin and forget. Or just find

an open leg of concrete and lay down for a sec. Most of the camp was nodding off, but I could see a fire spitting itself into the distance. So I stumbled toward the edges of this last web of closeness available, the kind where it's just bodies in proximity, but it's enough if you can make it be, and I could make anything plenty. That was what was beneath the fuck.

Unfucking the fuck to find enough there—this could have been a profound moment, but instead a man extended from the shadows and grabbed me.

It wasn't the first time I was raped, and I don't want what I'm about to say to diminish how dark a crime it is to attack the nexus of intimacy. But this time I loved it. It wasn't one of those fantasy come true situations—it's dirty and wrong so it's hot, like your groin is full of flaming pennies. It was heaven, ambrosia and harps, clouds turned to cream laced with cherries, whatever your image for heaven—this was mine, this rape. I couldn't really see the man's face. It was white, his skin was loose, the hairs around his penis were shaved and poked me in the delicate skin between belly and thigh. He pounded hard the way rapists do and I was crying, which got him more excited because he misunderstood the quality of tears on his hand as he dug it into my face, pumping harder. Until he moved it and I was able to tell him, "I love you."

His penis went soft because I took his rape away from him. So I backpedalled and gave him what he needed. Struggle. Because I loved him. I was so happy to be pleasing his again hardened cock that I started to laugh. I couldn't hold it in. "I love you I love you I love you," I rattled in spats. I was giggling, a child again, unable to tell a lie into the wide hips of our joined hearts. He collapsed beside me, slipping out in the slosh of my come. Not his. I turned my head to gaze at him. I'll never know if I was correct, but the face I saw through the sparkle of black, the flash of my match that went out and turned the world the momentary blue of parties, was the pale old face of the truck man. The air chest, the knowing I knew in the instant I saw that evil couple, that they had something special tucked inside the horror of themselves, a spiritual door, if you will. I know, I'm an atheist myself, but there's no denying the doors and the air chests. My lungs pushed down on my diaphragm, which pushed down on my belly, which pushed down on the pit of the womb in my womb and I couldn't breathe. I was a hysterical child, wailing with love, wailing hold me.

"Christ," he said and got up zipping. He ducked into the shadows. I tried to find him but he was gone.

We have words for this sort of thing to make it easier. "Stockholm syndrome." "Crazy bitch." The words function as envelopes, to hold the thing too unwieldy to look at straight. Like a body. My body holds in what no one will look at head on. No one could. The power of looking at a tree or a bumble bee can be blinding, so we wrap them in "tree" and "bumble bee" so we can get on with it. Go on, get on with it. But know that these women and men you believe to be trapped in delusion, a misrouting of neurons, strange, but then trauma is strange, so lets just call it something in order to pretend understanding, these women and men have looked their captor in the eye and loved him until it couldn't hurt. They don't care what you call them.

I don't care what you call me either, because I dropped through that trap door at the bottom of the bottom and came out on top. Power is circle we oval so vertical it appears line thin. I would offer a scene to show what happened when I stopped dropping, but I don't want you picturing me. I believe in messages of bliss slipped under the crack into the bottles of you, breadcrumbs in your wood, though. So I'm telling you my theory. You hate us night crawlers, we abject and dirty, beaten and poor and crumpled in admiration like dogs, or perhaps hate is too strong a word for the softer hearted of you, content to keep us folded like letters to be avoided most of the time, taken out of the package for the clean burn of pity now and then or to write a check, a form of hate, though isn't it, the tucking away, the signing?

My risk impulses took a sharp turn after the perfection of my story bookended in double rape like rainbows, look at that. Perfection. I didn't need them anymore. I'd conquered fear by becoming what gasps every heart, that fear in some nights that perhaps I am the lowest thing, the ugliest, the worst, most unwanted thing. I became it and found in every pocket of it nothing but blinding love. So I brushed myself off, knowing full well I'd reached my full potential and nothing could best me, and I won't tell you who I am, because you would be ruined by the knowing, but, my sweet puppets, you know me. I'm in your every living room, I'm there when you go to the bank, I'm blaring from your radio in traffic. Look, I'm there in your space right now, whether you want me or not. It's up to you whether to struggle. Every time you move you swell the coffers of my accounts. I would apologize if I felt sorry, but I don't. It's all here for you, blinding love—the way to win. Look straight ahead.

Pool.

all she had

A panel of grandfathers lived in the girl like a Greek chorus. One day she woke and they were building themselves
bleachers. After that they didn't do anything. Tired, they
complained. They shouted commentary about her choices
while they popped cold beers. They cracked themselves up
sometimes, especially when the girl tried to do something,
anything. They'd tease her about her hair and butt and forget
it if someone took interest in her. They'd be relentless about
the suitor's skinny legs or blank stare or intelligence quotient.
They liked the girl to keep still so they weren't jostled. If she
kept still enough they could grow quiet and take in the scen-
ery, frowning.

The girl at first tried to get them to leave by brute force,
that's it! She shook the benches to annoy them with rattle noises. "Ah look at this," they laughed, "The little weasel is showing

her muscles," and another one chimed in, "Have you been skipping the gym? You're looking a little droopy." So she stole his jacket. The grandfathers weren't very strong. She stole all of their jackets. They shivered and stared at her like wrinkled chimps. She held her ground for as long as she could.

She tried trickery next. She told them she knew of another young woman who loved to house grandfathers in her. She handed them pamphlets about how very still this other girl sits, how much Carnation Instant Breakfast she drinks, how often she reads the newspaper. She drew pictures of the imaginary girl's weak limbs. At first the grandfathers' eyes sparkled with interest. Then one asked, "Well, where does she live?"

"Oh, just up the way!" the girl answered.

"How will we get there?"

"It's just a short walk!"

"Walk?" Sniff. Sniff sniff sniff, down the line of Grandpas. Then laughter. "Walk!"

She knew she would have to try charm. The problem was the grandfathers had thinned her self-esteem. She was a waify wafer of a girl after all she had put up with. It wasn't easy hosting all these old men! She went to the store to find a dress. Outside in, she thought. A sales associate asked her if she needed help, and she began to cry. The grandfathers were annoyed at the racket. The sales associate too, was alarmed. The girl told her she needed help becoming as beautiful as she could. The sales associate had her doubts about the skinny young lady with the emotional display and stringy hair, but she knew an easy sale when she saw one, and besides, they were running a special. "We're running a special," the sales associate said. "Today is your lucky day."

Hordes of sales associates flocked to her carrying tea and rouge and brushes. They spritzed her and put stinging lip fatteners on her. They strapped shining leather boots on her, and wrapped her in cashmere. All the while the grandfathers shouted and sneezed. They teased her for looking like a clown. But even the grandfathers had to admit that when the sales associates were through, the girl looked pretty good.

They charged a lot of money, but this was fine with the girl. She paid and walked herself and the grandfathers into a bar. "It's loud in here!" they complained. She shushed them with three shots of scotch.

Several men stared at the young woman as she walked onto the dance floor. She made sure to curl the corners of her mouth just slightly at them, while keeping her face mostly deadened and mysterious. She thought about how this was too easy, why had she forgotten how easy this was? One by one, she asked the grandfathers if she could have this dance. She asked in the old fashioned way. Their wrinkly faces blushed, even the brown ones betrayed a little pink. It had been years since they had swayed to music. They resisted at first but soon the songs melted them and they rocked in place on the bleachers with their arms reaching off into the air. They imagined a form like the one they inhabited.

The girl made a request to the DJ, and her gracious swaying turned to thumping. Sweat stuck her skirt to her skin, her hair to her neck, and streamed. She stomped and stomped in her boots until her feet were bloody and the grandfathers were heaving and the bleachers broke. She ignored their screams as she turned inside out. It felt like plopping babies if babies were splinters and as long as a grandstand. The grandfathers slipped down her sides and clung to her feet. She kicked and kicked their sagging cheeks. They were a heap of broken bones and perspiration when she'd finally spent all she had. Other dancers were shouting, "Yeah girl." She walked out of the bar and inhaled the night alone—aside from the crumpled faces trailing behind her every step. She was exuberant. She'd rather drag their jingling corpses across dirty sidewalks forever than to hear another word.

Unfortunately they still managed to form words from their busted lips. They were difficult to understand, and so demanded even more attention from the girl. Her curiosity kept getting the better of her. The rising moans from the rattling grandfather pile trailed her like a smoking tail when she walked to class, to work, to the gym—*puff puff puff ugly puff puff fat puff dumb*. Furthermore, the broken bleachers lining her insides would get a chill in the evening. Frozen bleachers do a number on the lungs and heart, especially when the edges are crackled sharp. She couldn't expel the planks, however hard she danced, however hard she bore down on her diaphragm. The painful steps lived resolutely inside of her, a gravesite shaped like a pointed frown.

She heard laughter behind her and thought she knew what she had to do. "Come on," she said. "In you go." One by one she took them back inside, placing the grandfathers' shattered bodies onto the split bleachers. She balanced them on the far sides so that their weight held the fragile center of the construction together. For fun she shaped their skeletal frames into a tableaux of famous images such as *The Thinker*, the three monkeys who avoid evils, even Jesus on the stake. She noticed a few of them sneak smiles. She should have known that she'd made yet another mistake. From then on they were terribly quiet. She couldn't get a sound out of them if she tried, and she did. Their mockery was so complete; they had no need for words.

we win

Well and I thought, what kind of life would this be, really, if we must live the whole bloody mess of it without ever being able to enter the mouth of the beast? I felt this quite literally. I was an American now. It happened in a lake, spawn of things. Little fish were biting my ankles and giving me the heebie jeebies. The lake seemed to agree with me. The surface of it looked as if it had been given the chills. It was as if a hand had come down from above and tickled it. Now the lake was grossed out by its own innards, and so expressed it in waves and wakes like pimpled flesh. A female friend shared my disposition and said she wished she had a custom steel suit designed for lake going. This is how ideas are born. Yes, I thought. Not only could the nuisance of small things be protected against, but imagine the horrifying big things! And here lied my real interest—predation. Protection, you know, is costly. Upon reflection, though,

a steel suit would be unseemly. Too clunky. Too heavy. Too op-
posed to flotation. And there is the problem of the head. Oh,
the problem of the head.

It's jolly good I'm a chemist. I got my friends over at Basic Ten
to climb on board in the ideas phase. There needed to be some
plastic in the base. Bendability. Lightness. I thought, well, what
good would it be to create a suit that allowed safe entry into
the mouth of the beast if you couldn't happily slide around on
its teeth? So a certain slippery quality was necessary. At this
point I was still picturing a suit, some kind of metallic outfit.
Soon it became apparent that for the body to have maximum
agility in the face of the food chain it would need to be lighter—a sort of paint. Paint that conformed to the skin but con-
gealed into something impenetrable. The metals were added
and I'll tell you we had a heck of a time finding a chemical
process that would allow them to remain liquid without extreme heat. What good is a body paint that is too hot to touch
the skin? I won't bore you with the details. I will just say that
there are other ways to keep particles in motion and give you
a little wink.

After the first trial we realized that we had to adapt the formula. There was a snafu. Our substance was a feat of chemical
genius in many senses—it remained liquid in its can, it solidi-
fied upon contact, but remained bendable enough for all sorts
of physical prowess. (Not that our trial volunteers had much
of that—they were all crack heads, I think. I was disappointed
with our HR team in this regard.) Problems with removabil-
ity and skin rashes notwithstanding, it was simply a marvel,
even to its creators, but the problem was, well: jaws. Bengali

tigers and great white sharks (as just two examples of beasts) have truly unrivaled jaws. Not to mention incessant hunger. This is the whole problem with beasts, is it not? Most of them. Ours were useless if we fed them well! So even though our poor crack heads were able to slide all over incisors with glee, to stare into tonsils and punch them feeling no more than a pointy deep tissue massage while their mouths were open— problems arose when the beast decided to clamp down. It was terrible, really. No blood, but lung collapse, etc. Our whole production was nearly shut down. HR had done a good job in one respect—none of our trial volunteers had family lawyers coming after us or speaking to the press. These are the main things regulations worries about. By a hair we were able to keep going.

Have you ever bit down on aluminum foil? That's right. Beasts are no dummies. The problem of jaws was easy to circumvent. Easy in the sense that we knew the secret ingredient was aluminum and we had to go heavy on it. NOT EASY, I assure you, getting it in the correct proportions with the Basic Ten and other ingredients. A proper rubbery flexibility was vital. Was always at the crux of it. We had good minds on the team, though. Ex NASA and all that. There were military interests, of course. Unnecessary to mention but there's a lot of money there. Our next trial was set within a year.

It was amazing to behold. If you could have heard the peals of laughter from the participants! I almost wished I could risk a go myself. Imagine running your hands down the tongues of the most fearsome predators on all of our rolling rock in the sky! Staring into the dark shiny cavern of a throat without fear! That is until we got to the problem of the head. Beasts are no dummies. We've covered that. After ferociously shaking their prey around in their mouths with customary kill play, and recoiling with shrieks when they attempted to bite down hard, they ceased attacking. I'm talking specifically about the shark trial here. They swam around circling the participants. The absolute freedom the volunteers must have felt being able to play and splash one another smack in the middle of feeding grounds. Science at the peak of its beauty. But the damn things figured out that the heads were vulnerable. We hadn't painted their faces, obviously, and they were bitten clear off. Most of them.

The problem was essentially marketability. Would people buy a product that tore the skin off of their faces upon removal? I think not. Face skin is delicate, especially around the neck. There were already some snags in the sundress regarding successful removal of the product from the tough epidermis of the arms and legs. We tried everything. Baby powder. Thick lathers of lotion beneath the application. Most people lost some skin. At best they had a fearsome rash and quite a thorough waxing of body hair. Back to the lab it was. The legal hurdles were easier to jump with the excitement gathering. It was like being pressed up against the stage at Woodstock, or what is it, Coachella? So many screaming cheerers at your back.

We had to think outside of the box on this one. The skin just isn't amiable to liquid metals and plastics and rubbers. Or so went our thinking. I won't bore you with the details of giant post-it after giant post-it of our magic marker lockdown sessions. But finally it occurred to me simply, another nip on the ankle of my dream, this time Oceanside, while drinking my coffee on the wharf. Watching the seals. Skin doesn't have any native problem with the product. It is only with the product's removal. If I didn't pace the boardwalk all day recording voice notes into my Blackberry. I believe at moments I was leaping. At one point I went down to the harbor to pet the seals and kissed a gleaming coat.

We weren't coming up with a suit. We'd gone about it all wrong. What we were up to was nothing short of reinventing the body. Take that, Charlie D.! Take that, slow hand of time! We win. It doesn't have to come off, does it? In which case the head ceases to be a problem.

Now people are averse to change, but there are always the visionaries who are willing to go forth at the helm of any great movement. Starting with the folks who have no better choice, naturally, and then the eccentrics among the rich, and after that it's like dominos. Here fashion comes into play, and we did develop lines, the Coal Miner, the Cyborg, the Golden Child. As a happy byproduct, racism in the U.S. all but disappeared for a time. Dyes were applied and changed by plastic surgeons, tattoo artists adjusted their process, make-up underwent a dramatic reinvention and began to be used by males as well as females, the wig market exploded, cleaning and maintenance products were remarketed toward this new surface, in short: jobs were created. We called it Second Skin back then (Askin and Layer were lesser options) and with its accompanying assimilation, we finally beat the beast.

The first skins, it's uncomfortable to say, are difficult to look at now. They remind me of pink squirming baby mice, and I get a falling feeling in my anus. There are still some working poor who are uninterested. I must add here that it was years before I took the plunge myself. I myself had silly worries. But I have now stared down into the beast's belly and seen into the bloody swallow and heave of its fiercest muscle, been pressed and released and I have rubbed the teeth. I've tasted them and I have rubbed them with the silvery sheen of my perfect impermeability and there is nothing, nothing at all to be frightened of in the mouth of the beast.

haute culture

Being a porn star is really scary. One time I got all the way across town and realized I was still wearing my slippers. It was terrible, because I had to go back where I came from to get shoes. No place like home, I guess.

I'm not actually a porn star, I've only been in three porn movies so far and I think I want to stop now. The first one was a soft-core sex-positive lesbian foursome flick. The girl in charge was cool. I kind of admired her I guess. She was the art/activist type. None of the girls were drug addicts and it was pretty pleasant, really. In between shots we read magazines and acted like old friends. I'm not even a lesbian. But, you know, I'd been as much of a lesbian as every girl is in middle school, so I had no problems. In fact I missed it, softness, attention. Boys kind of suck that way sometimes, or they don't suck very well is maybe more accurate.

So that was fine, the first. But one of the girls in it gave me a phone number, and I was still curious. That was the driving force, curiosity. The money helped, I'm not going to lie. But really I just wanted to know what this thing was all about. I wanted to know if I liked it. I wanted to know who these people are that do things like this with their lives.

Well they're a bunch of drug addicts for the most part, it's true. It happens fast that someone gives you a bag, and it's New York City, so you're never quite in a real enough reality to think free drugs are a bad idea. You'll almost take free anything, even if you already stopped doing this kind of thing, like in my case. When you do drugs with people they are your instant besties, I remembered that from middle school too. Eventually, quickly, this kind of behavior leads you into forgetting your shoes. That's the part I forgot.

There were two worst parts of being a porn star. The first worst part was seeing my old theater teacher score a bag from one of the directors. Of all things it was ketamine she was doing. I mean, come on. You're an adult! At least do adult drugs if you're gonna do them. And the worst part of that worst part was that she tried to act cool with me. Like she was just the coolest old lady scoring bags from a bunch of teenage pimps and like we were in on the best secret together. I think I just stared at her. I wasn't even trying to make her feel bad—I just had no idea what to say.

The other worst part is even worse than the worst part of the first worst part. It was supposed to be my fourth shoot. Already, things had gotten darker. More disgusting kinds of acts were expected, like licking assholes, which I did not like, but I did it anyway. Surprisingly I liked when it was done to me.

I did like it sometimes. I was still new at it. I'm told that after awhile you never like it anymore. Unless you're a nympho and there are some of those. They don't fit in with the other girls. The girls were getting skinnier and skinnier and were grinding their jaws a lot. They were sticking out their lips like they thought they were fabulous. That's the cokeheads. The heroin addicts will just turn their heads and puke and then resume kissing you, eyes all rolled. So it was getting darker and I knew it, my stomach was feeling more and more uncomfortable, but like, I would just do a line too and that part was fun. Also, I was having the best conversations. These girls came from all over the five boroughs and some of them from really far away. Some were seniors in high school like me, some were even younger but they lied about it. Sometimes we would talk about lame things like how we feel about algebra, but also I found out about all of these weird parties. And I found out about all kinds of different Moms and Dads that exist and the kinds of things they cook, and so on and so forth. Sometimes it was sad and we would cry, but not all the time, and then we would play in the closet, put on sparkly things and redo our make up and do hairdos on each other and act like badasses in the mirror.

But on what was supposed to be my fourth shoot I arrived at what was really just a tent in an alleyway. It was one of those areas of the Bronx where nobody asks any questions and it's really far from the nearest subway stop. I was alone and I was high, so I kept looking around thinking I must be at the wrong place. But I peeled back a curtain, these thick dirty blankets, just to see and I will never get this image out of my mind.

It was a blond lady, real fake, you know? Bleach blond, white skin, giant boob job, and bright red lipstick. Her hair was teased like she never got over the eighties, but it almost just looked like she was crazy, like it was just messy. She was one of those dominatrix types, or whatever, that was the theme of the video. She had a whip and she was whipping this homeless guy. He was whimpering and trying to crawl away, but he was too far gone to really get anywhere. He was a big brown dude with hair stuck in one thick dreadlock. His clothes were completely falling apart. This wasn't a costume. He was the real deal. He was either touched in the head or a final stage drug addict, the kind that's going to die soon, you could tell. He had those enormous swollen ankles. All of him looked kind of swollen or he was just fat, but god his ankles. Like elephantitus. Plus the customary unlaced shoes with the backs bent down. There were two butt plugs on the little table where her drugs were set up next to her sunglasses, but when I peeled the curtain back, in that moment she was whipping him and jamming a giant hot pink dildo into his ass. She had this terrifying smile on her big red lips. Like she was mad at him and she probably was because maybe a part of her knew she was staring into the asshole of her possible future. The image made me feel like I'd suddenly gone to hell. The guy was muttering "please" and weeping but you could barely understand him because his mouth was maybe numb or something and she was saying real loud, "Yeah? You like to get fucked? Yeah."

I looked up to avoid the scene and caught the eye of the camera man and while it was not the worst part of the worst part, it almost was. You could tell he had no idea how his life had led him to this moment, this helpless watching. Those are the kinds of things you wonder. He half closed his lids at me and his jaw muscles moved like he was trying to bite his heart back down where it belonged. He turned his eye back to the lens, and I stuttered something about forgetting my shoes and I turned around and I ran.

free baby

Night.

Nougatine. There is nothing else for the moment but this Charleston Chew I found this morning. I hadn't seen one of these in ages, but in Brooklyn's eclectic range of shops, anything is possible. I put it in my bag for later and later is here. It's probably from 1983, but I am still eating it, with considerable trouble. I am looping the long strappy strips around my fingers cutting off their circulation. Pink chubby swabs stick out of their mummification. It's difficult to complete. Fat tulip fingertips stroke the foundling. She's lying on my legs, drifting. Given a child, what does one do but chew and mummify?

No tag, no note, no basket, or even a blanket swaddling her. Just these darting eyes like golden fish, reaching neck, rolling tub. Little licking mouth, chops. Where did that expression come from, the lips as chops?

The bridge of her nose is flat and wide, her golden fish eyes like a bird from hieroglyphs. Egyptian raven eyes—only cute. Sort of. An idea of cute. Forced to be seen as a gift, how cute can you be? I am a refugee camp.

Provisions. I eat the nougatine finger mummies. The blood drains back. I'm sticky. Alone.

Food, diapers, blanket. The rest can wait until tomorrow. I remember how to do this. When all else fails, sing. Burnt sugar skin, banana's foster skin. That edible baby thing, what did I read about that? Where is the instinct to phone a friend? In its place is this sighing feeling. A passive glitch in the matrix of my gut. I just want to wave my hand and say no bother. It's just me with a baby. No big.

But this is wrong. I will phone a friend. Put away the candy bar remains. Disassociate the baby from them. Call Gretch, Nyssa, Mom. Not Mom. Mom will make it a production. Mom will flip. Her wig will curl despite her not having a wig, she'll muffle the phone on her shirt and make wide eyes and hand motions at the boyfriend. Nyssa will count blessings, Gretch will judge. There is a little Charleston Chew left, briefly missing payphone days for their limited time, I take it back out and stick it in my mouth.

The Babies-R-Us in Union Square is closed. I stare back and forth at the greens of the surviving Barnes & Noble and the reds of the bank where Virgin Records was once. I want to go to a bodega, but there aren't any here so I decide to go back to Brooklyn. I take the subway. Through the turnstile she grunts but does not cry. I discover that she can hold her head up. I take the cue from her.

I stare at her the whole way, splayed again on her back

on my knees. My hands sweat, still sticky. My breath is short. The train goes above ground in Fort Greene and the golden spray of industrial buildings looks like a party. I imagine leaping from rooftop to rooftop, riding a trapeze, swinging down to grab joints out of people's mouths through the windows. I am not fit to be a mother.

But of course I won't be. There will be a procedure. Paperwork. It will be a hassle and sad, but that will be it. You don't just get free babies and keep them. This doesn't happen.

What would I teach her? I am a clay bowl. No soup. Only ridges smoothed down. I missed something along the way. I didn't learn whatever I was supposed to learn, and it goes deeper than gaps in my understanding of European History, or not having read enough Wittgenstein. I've learned nothing. Perhaps I've just forgotten. Being a Mother requires something. Something swollen. Something that if it were visual would appear like flickering lights over the ocean that would be made of truth. A belly of open hands. The kind of pictures greeting card artists paint. Or at least it requires a savings account. I clutch her feet. A lift in my body. I am flipping out, that's what I'm doing. It's our stop. I grab her up too quick from her supine position on my legs and there it goes. She begins to cry.

She cries as if she could write a new world if she is just loud enough. My heart thumps. What if I get arrested? She doesn't even look like she belongs to me. We don't match. Babies, do they scream like this with their real mothers? The wails are striking me right in the solar plexus. I shake and she shakes. My bag is slipping off of my back but I can't adjust it. I apologize to the local homeless man with my eyes as we flip through the turnstile. He smiles as always. Mouths the words "thank you" even though I haven't given him anything.

She's going to go hoarse. She punctuates the ends of each scream with a startling absence of breath, pushing hard against empty lungs. She craps. I hear it and feel the warmth. There was too much pressure bearing down. Instead of being grossed out I sympathize.

In my bodega, oddly, Isha is in and Mike is out. She doesn't often do nights. I sigh audibly when I see her and in the same instant, my eyes start streaming. I scold myself, but it's no use. I try to hide myself behind the baby, fixing my eyes on a stack of Fancy Feast cans.

Here is the beautiful thing about Isha: She says nothing. She picks up her long grabbing lever to grip a package of diapers from the top shelf, rips the pack open with one hand and grabs the baby from me with the other. It is experienced by the viewer, me, the rest of the store is deserted, as a single action taking all of three seconds. She lays a blanket down that has probably belonged to all eleven of her children. This is not hyperbole. Isha has eleven literal children. A Muslim thing I suppose. A belief in babies.

She lays her down and makes open mouth smiles. She shakes her head while she smiles. She coos up and down her vocal register. All the while she does this she does not break eye contact with the baby except once to check for shit stains on the last couple of wipes. The cries are getting softer. The diaper is changed. She picks her up and bounces her softly.

Now she looks at me.

She still says nothing, but her eyebrows ask the question.

"I don't know," I say. "Honestly. I don't." I shake my head and back up. Consider leaving the baby. I consider leaving the store and forgetting about her. Exactly like Vic had done to me in the auditorium. Like her Mother had done. Her Father had done. The school security guard who just snapped her gum and sucked her teeth when I told her that someone had left their baby at the show. Shook her head. Agreed to wait with me to see if she came back. Imagine: "Oops I forgot something." But then the guard just buried her head in her NY Metro. Ignored us both until everyone was gone and then stared us down. "You're gonna have to take her," she said.

As scared as I am, it occurs to me that there is nothing else. There really isn't anything else. So I just say. "I need formula and diapers." She pushes the opened pack toward me like she's moving a chess piece. She maintains eye contact and grabs an Enfamil.

"It'll be okay." She says.

This is a Mother.

I am a fire spinner and theatrical coach. By day I'm a trainer at P.N. Derns. I boycott everything but I take my trainees to an unnamed chain restaurant that we secretly love. They don't know I work circus parties at night. I'm rarely home before three AM.

Why didn't I go to the police station? Vic and I hit the bat outside during intermission, so I guess I was mildly stoned. I had imagined big gruff arms holding her all wrong, fingerprinting her, fluorescent lights—the opposite of holding her quietly breathing. But this is further proof: I just listened to the security guard. She said take her and I did. It seems like such a manic move now that I'm almost home. Where will I even put her?

I want to stay with Isha but it seems inappropriate. "Can I pay you tomorrow?" I ask. She waves her hand. She talks to me about sterilizing bottles. My breathing becomes a little short and I bolt out of there nodding.

Keys, baby, bag, table, light. I look at her. She smiles and I return it, automatic. Her lips and eyes are so glossy. She must be hungry. The bottle is new so I don't sterilize it. I open the package with one hand. I am trying to hold her with one arm while I pour the formula but it isn't working and I'm getting all hot in my chest and neck. She starts squirming and making little noises. I lay her on the couch, but I'm nervous she will fall off so I pick her back up, I tell myself to breathe but I don't. I figure it out. Coffee table. I'll make the formula on the coffee table while my body blocks her from falling off the sofa.

She sucks and sucks at the plastic nipple like it's the only and last plastic nipple that will ever be manufactured. She rubs the fabric of my sweater and stares into my eyes while she sucks. I am afraid she can see how dead certain corners of me are. Babies and animals seem to know too much, unhinged as they are from newspapers and e-mails and social networking. Instead, though, I feel alive in my corners. Her eyes are little suns. Jugs of positive energy or some such imaginary love seem to seep from her and pour over my face and down my head. I'm calm. She is too, her little suns are drooping, rolling back. Her lids come down and her mouth stops moving. Then she suddenly gulps air and startles herself, sucking and staring again. Repeat. She sleeps. Her hand comes undone from my sweater. Her fingernails are the prettiest pink drops I've ever seen. She vomits on me. Somehow this doesn't really wake her up. She falls back asleep.

There is no choice but to lay her in my bed, though this does not seem like a good idea. The goal is not to get attached. The goal is to be all Buddhist about it. First thing in the morning, call out of work, figure out where to bring her. I want to cuddle her and play with her toes, and this is not good. This is alarming. Why do babies do this to us? Where does this power come from? I mean, I'm not easily moved by smooth talking men, and I can resist chocolate when I must. Why am I unraveling so soft? I want to call my Mom but I don't want to wake her. I decide enough has happened for the day. I lay her in the center of the mattress and watch her while I remove the spit up sweater and slip a ripped t-shirt over my head and slide into my sweats. I move her to the corner by the wall so she won't fall off. I remember no pillows for babies, but I put her under the blanket. I lay on the other side of the bed. Just a baby guardrail, nothing else. Not a cuddler, mommy, or a friend even. But then she makes this noise in her sleep. It's ahahehoo, and I'm half in dream. It's a breathing sweet sound, sound. I go to her. I put my arms around her. Relaxation such as this has not happened since childhood maybe. I fall deeply asleep.

And then she wakes up screaming.

Repeat.

Morning.

By morning we are good friends unfortunately. There have been bottles, there have been songs. But I get dressed and wrap her up. I call my Mother over cereal, but decide not to tell her. I chew innocently. Tell her I love her. No tears, time to go, the day is brisk.

Why did I expect marble floors? The lobby is cramped, white walls, crappy linoleum, security behind bulletproof glass. I look at the board to the left, the directory. There are categories. There is not a category for lost and found babies. There is no baby drop-offery. I go with child services. Fourth floor. I present my ID. The baby is swatting my face. I bite her hand with my lips absentmindedly. The big dude signing me in smiles at me. "She's not mine," I say.

"She's cute," he says.

I agree with my eyes and lug the package of us into an elevator.

There is a sign in sheet here too. I sign in. We are both lulled by the television while we wait. My breathing gets soft. I wish to take a nap. She falls asleep for me. Our name is called. I get up carefully so she doesn't wake.

We enter a small office with one window looking into an alley and fluorescent strip lights. A frizzy haired woman, a Sesame Street safety maker with a blond spiral perm leans forward, again and again, looking up at me over her glasses as I tell her the story. She is who you go to if you have a splinter. Or need help organizing your bill book. A good woman, I think, I hope. I bite my fingers. My eyes bounce around the room while I tell her. I don't want to seem suspect, I don't know what the rules are regarding free babies, but I'm sure I have broken them. I don't want the baby to end up in the wrong place. I am irrationally afraid that this woman will just snatch her out of my hands in a sudden move. My throat pulls like a bent violin string. Jeesh, I better not cry.

The woman keeps rock-nodding, eyes wide, perma-nent smile. Fine hairs line her chin. Her nametag says Diane Lach.

"Um ... Ms. Lach?"

"Oh, and what is your name, Sweetie? I didn't get that, did I?" She pulls a post-it off.

"Chloe."

"Ok, Chloe...?"

"Field." My name sounds over bright.

"Great. Yes, Chloe."

"Can I be involved in her adoption process, do you think? Can I, do I have any rights..."

"Why don't we measure her? Huh? Get her fingerprints."

"Because I don't want her to go to just anyone."

"Oh there are just lovely families. So many lovely families waiting to adopt. They like newborns, but she's still very young. She'll go. She shouldn't need a foster."

My stomach flips. I expected something else. I expected to be told to go to at least five different offices, the police station, fill out scores of forms, be subjected to questioning. The lack of bureaucracy I've come to expect is frightening. Do people really flip free babies like this? Pass her on, no big. She'll go. Ms. Lach reads my mind.

"Of course she'll have to be brought down to the clinic, get blood work. Make sure everything checks out." Something at least. But "checks out" rings, repeats in my brain. They mean drugs, they'll check her for drugs.

"What if her mother comes looking for her? What if she changes her mind?"

"Oh they don't, Hon. They don't," she says.

I don't like this woman's mouth. It's square. Everything about her seems like it could just peel off like a zipped costume to reveal an inside that is something else entirely. I stand up.

"You know on second thought, maybe I should take her to the police," I say. She blinks three times. "I just don't feel right, I mean, I teach at that school. What if the mother comes back?"

Diane rock-nods and square mouth smiles. "You could do that if it makes you feel better." She hands me a tissue. "They'll just send her back here eventually, though. And I don't like those cribs there at the police station. Dingy." They have cribs at the police station? Everything is swimming. I discover that I want to keep her. I fall back into my chair.

"What if I keep her for now, you know, like a foster. Just for now." I am shocked by myself. The baby is looking up at me sucking her lips and fingers. I don't ever want to be away from her, ever, but then for just a half of a second I want to drop her on the ground for causing me this anguish.

"There's no need. She'll go. She's pretty. If she was fostered for too long it would ruin her chances." I blow my nose. Squeeze her. She burps. "Chloe, you're young. What did you say it was you did for a living again?"

"I'm a fire spinner. And I juggle too." I see her eyebrow and want to punch it. "But I also work for P.N. Derns and teach." I remember that I hate these people. These spinster desk ladies with their framed pet photos. Safety maker my ass. Bill book my ass. I stand up again.

Afternoon.

Another waiting room. Nya, I've started to call her, Nya, is lying on my knees and I'm teaching her to clap hands. I'm holding her hands and clapping them for her. Every time she smiles my eyes and throat drip and clench, burning. But I smile back. These government buildings, they have everything. We are in some sort of clinic now. Other women are waiting and I can't figure out their positions. Are they giving babies up or getting them? Are they just people without health insurance? Is this like a Planned Parenthood for babies? I can't tell. Everyone is quiet with their magazines. CNN is on mute. I am here to give away a baby, that's all I know. She's been measured and printed. Lach has promised that they will do a search for her mom, check if her prints match any local hospital records. I am unclear on the instructions. I don't know where we go next after the doctor. I suppose they will tell me. This is all very confusing. Yesterday at this time I was rehearsing with my tenth graders. They were not spitting out their gum and cracking each other up and I was telling them a Helen Keller quote. "It's okay to have butterflies in your stomach. The trick is to get them to fly in formation." They were staring at me either blankly or with the high-octane teenaged love that during stage fright busts up eyebrows normally locked in the raised position.

Nya starts fussing. I give her the bent knuckle of my pointer to chew on. It's ok because I've sanitized my hands three times today out of boredom and an abundance of Purell pumps on desks and counters intended for social service. She grabs my hand with both of her tiny ones. She shakes her head a little, like no.

Our name is called. I grab our paltry stuff and follow a woman with red streaks in her twist. I watch her gold hoops swing against her neck. She turns her head.

"I'm Asia," she says.

"Chloe."

"Pleasure. She's cute isn't she?"

"Yes," I say and put my head down on the thin hairs that coat her skull. She smells like formula. I feel her soft spot pulse beneath my closed lips.

Asia leads me into a tiny cramped room with a desk. It looks like it was once a custodial closet. She reaches out her hands and takes Nya from me.

"I'm gonna go ahead and take her to the examining room. You can wait here." My arm shoots after her and I am embarrassed so I fix my hair with it in a gestural joke no one sees and sit. It is a long time before Asia comes back. I watch a tiny digital clock. Probably the most boring activity in the world. There are no books in the room, just some pamphlets about various health concerns like SIDS and AIDS. The desk is messed up. It's got stacks and stack of papers on it. There are dust bunnies next to the green garbage can, like someone missed. My ass starts hurting from all of the day's chairs. My arms feel light and my chest a little too cool like it's naked without Nya. I notice my knees. I think they are kind of cute. I'm in the mood to have fire in my hands and mouth. I wonder what other people are doing right now. I sing a little, in the quietest octave above a whisper. I have a memory. My back on a table and my legs in the air, performing the hisses of childbirth with my friend Moira spitting flames from underneath, between my legs. We called the act "Baby" and everyone loved it. Now it seems profane and also true. I taste ethanol in my mouth, smoke pain in my lungs, the undeniable desire to hurt a little bit, as if enough little bits of hurt will stave off the big chunks that hunt from the horizon. I imagine little cups in a line of wire along my shoulder blades running down both of my arms. The cups are filled with kerosene and spotters torch my back and arms, the flames shooting high as I flap. Angel, I'll call the act. Or Nya. Night.

Asia comes in.

"Okay, that's it," she says and makes a motion like dusting off the hands.

"Hmm?"

"You can go home now. The baby is fine."

"What?"

"Everything checked out, she's perfectly healthy, no addictions, we checked her into the nursery." Like the Ritz. Or the Carlton. I cry. I just finally cry.

"I want to say goodbye," I barely get it out. I'm drool crying. "Can't I say goodbye?"

"It's better if you don't. It's better if you don't." She said twice. Twice.

Night.

songbun song

Hyo washes his hands in hot water. He presses his nails into his cloth to remove each excess drop to ready his fingers for pinning. The baby fusses but falls back to sleep, dreaming, her arms up. Hyo tweezes his find identified easily as Thyas Juno by the orange under markings. He removes it from the aspirator and fumigates it, lulled by its increasingly tranquil spasms. He chooses a spot next to an inferior twin but the spacing in the display box is wrong. He moisturizes the smaller specimen avoiding its antennae, swabbing it with alcohol for repositioning. The radio is on. Kim Jong Un reminds us again that he has met with a famous basketball player Rod Man and they created a great friendship. Praise the Supreme Leader.

In the dream round shapes come toward her, glowing gray. She reaches.

Hyo steps outside, placing each of his feet in a slipper while the solution takes. Hyo is grateful for his transfer to Yoduk. A shock of gold corn weaves into evening sun, like the drool of a sky with mountains for a head. He displayed great self-reliance when his wife Eun died and he never missed a day of work. His fists clench involuntarily and he concentrates on unfurling them. Trains the pitch of his eyes on the marsh, really a puddle from the intense rains, where he'd found a Nehalennia Speclosa today after spitting in the mouths of a pair of dogs. He'd caught them kissing and thought to pigeon them when he heard the signature drone and spotted the delicate blue tipped tail. He had his kit so the kissers got off easy. He rubs his hands together and snaps his neck to release his shoulder.

She wakes with a start because she can't breathe. It's the squares again. She hates the edges. She finds her belly noise.

The baby starts crying. How Hyo loves his daughter. Little Ko. Hana, Hana, in public, but in private he named her after The Great Mother. He does not know how to deal with the crying fits Ko is lately prone to, however. He yells for Hee Young. When she doesn't come he crosses the dirt street between his officers compound and the first line of huts to the one she shares with her husband and three kids. He walks in without knocking. There is no door anyway.

Hee Young sees Officer Hyo enter her hut and in a single motion covers her cheeks and breasts with her tangled hair and her infant son's face with his moth eaten blanket. Her gut clamps. Burp. Stand. She knows she may earn a reward when Hyo comes, but the reward of feeding her child is greater. She's uneasy on her legs. The pull of her babies is too strong, it's thrumming in her ribs. At least she's sure her neighbor will check on them. Last week she gave the other mother a cherry candy from Hyo's house.

Hyo keeps clear of the cracked and teeming walls of Hee Young's hut, hugging himself. He doesn't want to catch an infestation of lice and fleas. As it is Hee Young can never disrobe enough for his comfort when summoned into his officer's quarters. She is breastfeeding her youngest in the shadowed corner. The oldest girl is out working of course, but her three year old looks starved to near death on a mat in the corner, his face swaying in the throes of fever. "Why do these people insist upon reproducing?" Hyo thinks. They hadn't caught Hee Young's pregnancy in time for the abortion injections to work. The birth was difficult. The slow recovery has rendered the woman practically useless to the camp. Hyo protects her from the others, though, because of her inconsistent gift for quieting his daughter Ko. Among other inconsistent gifts. Hee Young should be thankful. She scrabbles to her feet before he can slap her. He admonishes her for not hearing his calls but she is already at the door gathering her skirt in a thick clutch in front of her.

Hee Young keeps her eyes low to avoid gazes that find the holes in her clothes no matter how much she gathers them to cover. She doesn't want to see the fainted workers scattered on the dirt path either, though, so she raises them again to look straight ahead. They are already nearing the proper houses where the officers live with their grasses. Pavements and gates. She looks forward to sights of clean suits or a glimpse of a fat child huffing with the pink cheeks of play, her favorite delight above all, even birds or sugar.

Hyo understands hard work. Once he had been coal miner, most noble Songbun, though he was terrible at the job, and wound up running the company accounts instead. No one knew that, though it could be found out that his wife was from a family of elite scientists. He was lucky for this job. Bad Songbun, but his wife had saved him, inadvertently, by dying. The erasure of the undiscovered wealth-stained lineage, and the kneejerk pity taken on a single father rescued him. He would trade it all for one more minute touching one warm finger of her, but what impure thoughts. How ungrateful. He pinches the scabbing skin between his thoughts discreetly as he walks and then his inner thigh through his pocket until he winces.

He types his identification to set the alarm system. The marvel of beeps.

Once in the house, Hee Young goes to baby Ko and Hyo goes to even his moth twins in their glass case. To calm himself he plucks a leg from the Acromantis Japonica mounted upside down at the base of the box. Then another, and another. Leg. Leg. It's a symmetrical destruction he allows himself, the only one he allows, in his otherwise impeccable craft of preservation.

She takes air in for another push on her belly noise. The footsteps of the big ones sound like accidents.

It's the emptiness he loves about the insects; so empty their husks practically vibrate with it. Perfection of stillness.

She makes it say go and no in her noise.

His daughter is still screaming. For her mother, Hyo knows. The howling began last month when her mother passed. She is too young to understand, he reasons, but the timing is uncanny. Maybe distress is Ko's natural state and his wife had somehow dammed the outpouring before with the small boulder of her maternal body. Hee Young brings the baby in, her sagging breast pocked with scars, the infant's mouth refusing the nipple.

Ko shakes her face and twitches her hands open and closed like a pincher crab. She's grabbing for the other part of her but can't find it again. She doesn't want a tit now, not this tit. Not warm, not sweet, not milk. "Not," she cries in non-speech. The shapes circling her are the wrong shapes again. The not.

Hyo turns his head and plucks another leg. Peels it slow and with great care, holding it up to the sunset light beneath the shade to behold peaks of hair, edges of transparency. Sing, he tells Hee Young without turning his head, the song of the eternal president. Sing *No Motherland Without You*, he challenges. His voice comes out hoarse. He is suddenly urgent with his need for the woman to sing. He swings toward her but deadens his eyes at her graying face. Hee Young's reeducation is pointless—her family defected. Her parents had been lawyers and her sentence was life for three generations, but perhaps the tune would soothe Ko. *Sing*, Hyo's jaw, his chin and hand say, and Hee sings.

Ko wails.

Her father snatches her back. Sticks the cleansed mantis in her tiny grip. Hee Young shakes her head. The baby drops the carcass and Hyo points with his toe for Hee Young to clean the tile beneath it. He detests mess. He dabs his daughter's palm with a cotton ball.

Hee Young hates the smell so close to Hyo's crotch, the smell of the rat meat they must eat to fight infection. Worse than rat meat, rat meat and feet and bleach. Sickness. Shame. His badge dangles from his belt. She deflates like a straw has sucked her through. Breath leaving the eyes. She wipes the pristine floor with a wet rag, picking at the scattered legs, shocked by how light the bug's midsection is. Like it holds less than air. She stifles a strong instinct to put it in her mouth and instead fills her cavity with the melody she is remembering against Hyo's glare that says she won't. Hunger will push a memory heavy as a freight train forward with one hand. The radio is still on. Words emerge as backdrop. Merciless. National Reunification. National Desire. This man, Officer Hyo, has a pulse of kindness like stray static zaps in the form of treats sometimes. She falters her voice for pity, a prayer for sweet.

Ko wails along for an emptiness she understands in not understanding, absence in immaculate ache. As loud as wrong birth she screams to Hee's grave rendition of
No Motherland,
Ko the Coda sounding
Without You,
soprano.
Hyo hears the timbre of elegy and joins,
If the world changes one hundred times,
pinching his softest skin again he grunts repetition of the start,
Cannot exist,
the squeeze cuts, percussion pushing for finale,
Without you,
stuck between notes, glissando of Hee and Ko, the loop of the chorus in blood.
All three sweat.

Embarrassed by his dripping thigh and eyes, Hyo returns to his station by the window to cap his solutions. Ko's red cheeks make sucking motions as she comes to rest. Despite herself Hee Young rises to check on Hyo but notices the unwatched dish of cherry candy and the baby calming and refrains. *If the world changes*, she sings alone, slipping her free hand into the bowl.

corner

I ate an entire terrycloth bath towel. Are you going to jump and raise your hand in the air and say, *Oh me too! Me too!?* I worried I would gain weight. So I started pulling it out by the last dangling corner in my throat. I gagged around every millimeter and my hands were covered in drool and tear drops. You caught me heaving with two inches of towel hanging out of my mouth and you shook your head. Got your boyfriend to hold my shoulders back. You got a good grip. The towel was orange and full sized. Not a beach towel, mind you, but big enough to wrap and tuck and be covered after a warm bath. It was dry when I ate it but wet coming out. Hot bile rose to each tug. My mouth was a snail shell. You were good, better then I thought you would be. You remained concentrated. Quiet. Once you got it going you pulled hard and half the towel came out in one terrible yank. I screamed through my nose. *Why did I eat this towel?* I thought. And, *Thank God for my mother.* There was still a good bit in my stomach. I could feel it coiled in acid like a hairy snake. The urge to vomit was what I imagine the urge to push in childbirth would be. But the puke wouldn't come out because it got soaked up as it rose and blocked. The true definition of dry heave—the quicker picker upper. You pulled more out but left the last bit lodged and left the room. You must have known what would happen when the last corner, the one with the tag, was finally out.

check and chase

Their house was playing tricks on them. Check and Chase Jones were twins not hailing from the same zygote. They had, as they liked to say, their "own sperm," yet were nonetheless joined in their zeal for toys and a mutual hope for a stepfather with his own DS system. But Check and Chase were losing things. They had noted the occasional trend since perhaps as early as six years old. Check had anyway, he was the first-born and the bigger, dominant twin. A wooden block was lost here, a Candy Land piece there. Practically every toy distributed by Charity Santa was missing an integral part by January. This was standard annual operating procedure. But things had grown worse since their tenth birthday. Even Chase could see it. The house had turned on them.

A train set had come down the chute this year, a birthday present from their uncle. It was a silly antiquated toy, Check thought, a dream come true, Chase thought. But it didn't matter what either of them thought because one week into July the entire train set had disappeared.

"It's an abomination!" Check shouted with his fist in the air. "Mommy! Why don't you ever clean the stupid house!"

He stomped down the stairs, Chase following with her blanket, chubby tears plopping off her cheeks.

"For real!" Chase echoed. "Why?"

Mom didn't answer of course. She was still sleeping, as usual. She would wake up around one and light a joint. It was important that they caught her in her brief groggy moment of sobriety if they had questions. But it was only ten in the morning. They had a long way to go. Check felt it was important that he and Chase devise their own plan. Mom could not be counted on. For all they knew, she and the house were in cahoots.

The kitchen was falling into disrepair. Like all of the rooms of the house, it was steeped in squalor, plump with rot, bursting with broken bits of useless items.

They had a "hutch" that sometimes hid lost things behind piles of unopened mail and plates of rotting burger and brownies. Almost anything imaginable could be found stuffed inside of this piece of furniture if you were brave enough to shuffle things around. Socks, stuffed animals, commemorative paperweights. Check had a hunch that a train set could not hide on the hutch—too big. But Chase wanted to search it anyway. It had been a prime hiding spot for the house in the past, and Chase could not be dissuaded. She yanked a garbage bag from a bag of bags and dragged it up to the lowest shelf. She chucked things into it without mercy. "Why does she have a horse doll that's missing a head and a leg!?" She shook the aforementioned object at her brother and dumped it into the bag.

"Mommy's gonna be pissed if you throw that away." Check said. Chase glared at him. "I'm just saying," he said, throwing his hands up in the air for dramatic innocence. "I don't think the train set is in the hutch."

"Yeah well maybe your Transformer is in here. And anyway it's disgusting. And anyway you never know with this house." She was scooping up whole piles of mail and throwing them in the bag.

"That's Mommy's bills," Check said.

"She doesn't pay them anyway," Chase said. "She has the numbers in her phone. She'll call for more time or Grandma will pay them."

"True," Check agreed. "But she'll be mad if it's clean and she can't find her stuff."

"I don't GIVE A CRAP!" Chase shouted.

This outburst was a role reversal. Usually Chase was the sweet twin. She still sucked her thumb and her brown eyes were shaped like sideways tears. She was the one who held their Mother's hair if she was throwing up, defended her when Check's eyes became hot metal brands, the only one who could talk her brother down from his plans for an all out coup. But she was going a little nuts today. She was at her wits end.

Check needed to calm her down if they were going to puzzle out the secret of the house.

"When does the cheddar come?" he asked.

"Why do you always gotta try to sound street?" Chase said, rolling her eyes. "Anyway nobody says that anymore and you're smart so why don't you act like it?" No answer, just foot switching from Check, so Chase continued. "It's the middle of July, right? It comes on the first. She probably already spent it all."

She was right, unfortunately. The fridge and pantry were stuffed with such pleasantries as squirtable cheese, fruit gushers, devil dogs, hot dogs, frozen waffles, hot pockets, potato chips, and generic cola. That meant the check had arrived and that it wouldn't last the whole month. The first and second weeks were always the best.

"I think we need to buy a safe." Check said.

Chase looked up at her brother. His curls were all haywire. He had some crust dried on his cheek, which was darker than hers, the color of cardboard in the rain. His body lurched in fits and starts because he was thinking. He smelled like socks, but he had a point. "I want to find the train set," she whined anyway. She loved that train set. It had metallic red doors that really opened.

"I know you do," he placed his hand on her shoulder, "But the fact is, Chase, that our house eats things. Our first strategy should be defense. Once we have that down we can think about offense."

"The house will probably eat the safe." She put her forehead on her arm. "Why does our house hate us?"

"It doesn't hate us. It's just hungry, I guess." Chase stopped with that line of thinking because he didn't like the Pepto Bismol coated feeling of it. "It's just so messy which is Mom's fault." He didn't like that line of thinking either. He went back to basics. "The safe will need to be big and we'll have to hide it."

"Bigger than a train set? That will be expensive. Where do you even buy a safe? The bodega don't have no safes."

"True," Check said, rubbing his chin. "Maybe at Target?"

"Target is too far. That's two trains and I hate riding the A."

Check hated riding the A too. For some reason, all the scary people preferred the A. And it smelled bad. People were always taking shits in it. But then he had an idea.

"Maybe Miss Reynolds will take us!"

"Oh man, Check. I hate that lady. She'll make us cat sit. I'm allergic to her cats. Plus she talks bad about Mom."

"Yeah but she has a car. Who else do you know who has a car?"

"True," Chase agreed as she threw away a thousand piece puzzle with only three pieces clattering in the box. She scanned the room again, her eyes just innocent enough to imagine that her train set might reappear somewhere she'd already looked a hundred times. Instead she saw the "curtains" (dirty sheets) falling off of the wall. The corner shelf was piled with junked clothes and old cookie tins stacked on an unopened box of kitten plates from the dollar store. She looked at the blackened linoleum coming up and the gummy crust between the slots of the drop table. The two door-less cabinets beneath the sink revealed piles of food and dishes like its underwear were showing. There wasn't a dent in the mess in the hutch in front of her, though her bag was almost full. A dirty blind fell from the window bringing the curtain with it and a fat roach plunked onto the floor as if the house was responding to her. As if it was saying screw you, Chase. Quit your whining. She sighed. Her arm stuck to the table with dry grape jelly adhesive, but she tore it free to rub her eyes.

"What about the white kid?" she asked.

"He don't have a car. He's an artist," Check said by way of explanation. "Besides we shouldn't keep being seen with that white kid."

"Gringo, our Mom is white."

"No she's not. She's half Puerto Rican."

"No, she just says that."

"Why would she lie about being Puerto Rican?" Check asked.

"Because Yarelis says it's better than Dominican and you have to be something in Bed Stuy. But that white kid is nice."

"Yeah but her hair is black, and so are her eyes. Anyway people would know if she wasn't Puerto Rican."

"Not in this neighborhood. Everybody is Jamaican or Black. Anyway you ever heard her speak Spanish? You ever hear Grandma speak Spanish?"

"She says papi and she says pen day ho."

"Everybody says that. Anyway Grandma told me. She's not Puerto Rican, Check. I hate to tell you."

Check didn't know what to say at the moment. He hated being proven wrong and he hated when his Mom was caught in a lie. He hated that white people were moving to Bed Stuy (because everyone knows what that means—you're just two steps away from the Bronx where Jamir said people will beat you just because they don't like your eyebrows) and he hated that him and his sister and their baby brother were half white instead of a quarter. Or a whole, but screw that. He hated all the filmmakers and comedians and musicians that made his neighborhood famous. He wanted it to be invisible. He re-membered seeing the camera crews when he was little. He remembered waving at the people in crisp clothes, and them not noticing, talking into shiny cell phones and walkie talkies. He paced the kitchen, balling his hands into fists. He pushed an empty cup off of the table. Chase met his eyes without making any sort of face.

Then he knew he was acting like a stereo type, like they learned about in Miss Terry's class. Acting like a stereo type makes you invisible, she taught them. He had pictured becoming just a sound blaring out of a car. He didn't want to be an invisible car stereo noise, so he tried the breathing she taught him. Quietly, so Chase wouldn't hear. Then he got mad because everyone should be able to be angry when something is wrong, but then he had to start the breathing again, because he still didn't want to be a stereo type, even if things were wrong and he thought maybe if Bed Stuy could just get angry instead of him, it would become invisible enough and they could stay. Then he thought of something else, a question. He looked into the center of his sister's four kite-shaped freckles.

"If Mom lied about being Spanish do you think it's true that our dad died in Iraq?" Check whispered.

Chase looked up like answers could fall. She closed her eyes and nodded.

The upstairs creaked, but Mom wouldn't be up yet. The baby probably woke up. Just in case Check asked, "Did anybody sleep over last night." Chase looked over and shook her head no.

"I didn't hear anything."

They went upstairs dodging piles of clothes, papers, and baby toys on the steps. The house never ate Carter's toys. There always seemed to be lots. Dirty colored plastic with its sweet yellow smell abounded on the stained floors.

They opened the door to the bedroom the three of them shared. Carter was up, playing piano on a tiny broken keyboard. He looked up and held his arms out. "Chay Chay," he said smiling.

"I'm not picking you up right now, Cart. We have important things to do."

But Carter toddled over to give Check a hug. Carter loved Check. He loved Chase too, but he wanted to *be* Check. When it sunk in that Check wouldn't pick him up he toddled over to Chase and leaned his head into her thigh. He stretched his arms out and yelled, "Uppy? Uppy?" Chase picked him up.

"Come on," she said. "We gotta change this diaper and you're gonna watch cartoons."

"No," Carter said, but was ignored.

Once Carter was situated on the couch with a plate of dry cheerios and a bottle, lying among the empty DVD boxes, stale popcorn and ever abundant piles of dirty clothing, Check and Chase were free to face the betrayal of the house again. They popped in Adult Swim for Carter and pressed play.

"Isn't there an attic?" Chase asked.

"No dummy, it's just a crawl space." Check was back in a foul mood.

"Well shouldn't we check it Checko?"

"We need a ladder. We don't have a ladder. We need to focus. We need to get a safe," Check said, but he was staring at the television, absently stroking Carters hair. All three of them sighed intermittently while hyperactive lights changed the colors of their faces.

"We'll have to steal some money then. A lot of money. Last time Mom knew and that was only five dollars," Chase said, but she too was loosing interest. She held Carter's little foot and stared ahead.

"She thought that guy stole it from her."

"Yeah but there's no guy here today."

"True."

They became lost in the television. They loved Aqua Teen Hunger Force. Frylock was Check's favorite, but Chase was partial to Meatwad. Carter just liked the reds, blues, and greens.

They picked cheerios from Carters plate and settled deeper into the couch, watching and wondering. Chase wondered if the starving house would eventually eat them. Her finger circled the rough plastic edge of a burn on the arm of the couch. Check wondered about life in the Bronx, if they were really so tough over there. He slipped his left sock off with the big toe of his right foot and flicked it across the room. Carter wondered when his older brother and sister were going to stop stealing his cheerios. He swatted at their hands and squirmed belly first.

The house wondered why these kids were such pussies. It felt it deserved competitors of greater merit. These kids were practically feeding it their toys. The house hoped that Carter would grow up to be a worthier opponent. It decided to start consuming his possessions a little earlier on in his development. It had, perhaps, spoiled the twins. The house searched itself for something that would be properly missed.

Mom wondered nothing because she was face down on torn sheets, dead asleep. Her leg hung off the edge of her crooked bed. Her hand still clutched a cigarette that had long gone out. She dreamed of a train set.

(impasse)

no, go

Nogo© privacy software has been successfully downloaded to your computer ✓

Thank you for downloading Nogo©, revolutionary new software designed to protect the privacy of consumers like you. You will: never again worry about target marketers combing your e-mails for word keys to your identity. You will: eliminate the e-mail and social networking equivalent of the "drunk dial" from hindering the progression of your social life. You will: maintain an aloof persona in all of your traceable, searchable, readable inter(net)actions. You will: never again type a revealing word (subject for all time to public scrutiny), without Nogo© having its say. It's your life—your will.

Please take a moment to browse through our PREMIUM ED-
ITING SERVICES, affordable and easy to add, simply click
on the options listed below to learn more and download such
features as LIVE EDIT—where professional writers, ex CIA
agents, and psychologists are available 24/7 to discuss safe
word and phrase options with you, PSYCOANALYTIC FIL-
TER, which screens your text for words that indicate that your
unconscious may be piping up without your consent, and LIT-
ERARY GENIUS, a filter that checks your inter(net)actions
for clichés, sentimentality, overly contemporary references,
and changes in tense and point of view. We hope you enjoy
Nogo©—Your internet experience will never again be riddled
with yourself.

Continue with BASIC SERVICE ONLY ✓

Proceed to e-mail ✓

Compose Message:

Dear Sandy,

I am writing this message because I'm very **[Literary Genius has something to say! Add Literary Genius?] [Liter-
ary Genius has been ignored]** extremely? **[Literary Genius
has something to say! Add Literary Genius?] [Literary
Genius has been ignored]** I'm perturbed, Sandy. **[Basic
service suggests replacing the word: upset. The word:
upset has been replaced with the word: perturbed.]** It's
time we have an adult **[Basic Service does not recommend
adult content]** jesus! **[Basic Service recommends replacing the word: jesus! Suggested replacements include:
darn it!, good gracious!, oh my!, Basic Service has**

been ignored.] Conversation about our child. [Psychoana-
lytic filter has something to say. Psychoanalytic filter
has been ignored.]

Are you sure you want to exit this screen?
Message has been saved ✓

Basic Service filter has been changed to: Low

Return to message?

Are you sure you want to: Erase all Nogo© comments?

Nogo© comments have been successfully erased ✓

Dear Sandy,

I am writing this message because I'm very extremely? I'm perturbed, Sandy. It's time we have an adult jesus! Conversation
about our child.

Basically I'm mad [Live Editors wish to chat with you. A
free 30 day trial is being offered to new customers like
you! Invite Live Editors to chat?]

A free 30 day trial of Live Edit ™ has been successfully
added to your account ✓

Beverly says:

Hello Mr. Brooks. When you say "mad" here, what do you mean?

Harrison says:

Angry, Beverly. Angry. And I know I shouldn't tell my ex-wife I'm angry with her when we're in a custody battle. But I was getting frustrated by these constant interruptions.

Beverly says:

Your wife interrupts you?

Harrison says:

What? No. We're divorced. I only accepted live edit so I could ask someone how to stop this program from notifying me when the additional features have something to say.

Beverly says:

Do you have a hard time accepting feedback, Mr. Brooks?

Harrison says:

I signed up for the damn thing, didn't I? It's just, it's every other word!

Beverly says:

Are you prone to hostility in general?

Harrison says:

No, BEVERLY, but I don't have all day to compose an email. I just want to make sure that there's nothing in my correspondences with her that could be brought up in court. My lawyer recommended the service.

Beverly says:

As you get used to using Nogo it becomes easier to predict what it will take issue with. It will hardly interrupt you at all.

Harrison says:

Beverly, can you just help me make it so the premium services will stop being offered? Is it in my preferences?

Beverly says:

Well if you add the premium services you can turn all of their filters on low. You'll hear from them less often then.

Harrison says:

You're telling me I have to pay the extra money to shut them up? What a scam!

Beverly says:

You are projecting a lot of anger, Mr. Brooks.

Harrison says:

What?

Beverly is typing...

Harrison says:

Beverly, no offence but can I please talk to a different live editor?

Beverly says:

You can lead a horse to water but you can't make him drink.

Harrison says:

What?

Beverly says:

A bird in the hand is worth two in the bush.

Harrison:

That doesn't even make sense, Beverly. Literary Genius has something to say.

Beverly says:

People are strange, when you're a stranger.

Harrison says:

Fine. If you won't give me another editor, can I talk to a manager?

Beverly says:

Sure, Mr. Brooks. Another editor will be available in a few minutes. But if you continue doing the same things you'll get the same results.

Compose Message:

-seeing
-what
-happens
-if
-it's
-put
-another
-way
-word
-tests:
-resulting
-moonpack
-elevator
-sky
-ditty
-paced
-wife
-never
-showed
-up
-with
-son
-again

-waiting
-wren
-prunes
-grit
-sticks
-shadow
-twin
-ten
-years
-manipulating?

HA! Maybe that Beverly card was right [Basic Service recommends replacing the word: weirdo. Suggested replacements include: card, eccentric, original.]

-Fine,
-Nogo.
-I'll
-write
-in
-lists
-damnit!!!

-Dear
-Sandy
-I
-wish
-your
-hair
-would
-burn

-off
-and
-you'd
-have
-to
-eat
-it
-dipped
-in
-lard
-and
-fried
-with
-asparagus
-piss
-I
-want
-my
-son
-you
-jacked
-up
-piece
-of

> Jason says:

> hello Mr. Brooks. need help with Nogo?

> Harrison says:

> Yes! Jason? Hi I'm relegated to typing lists here to avoid these premium filters.

Jason says:

yeah, i'm sorry dude. it's annoying, right?

Harrison says:

Yes! It's very annoying.

Jason says:

totally blows.

Harrison says:

Indeed it blows. How do I get rid of them?

Jason says:

who? your wife and kids?

Harrison says:

What? No. I mean, I wouldn't mind getting rid of my wife, but I mean the interruptions.

Jason says:

yeah, i, uh, i been hearing that a lot today. to be honest, it's only my second day on the job. i think they have some kinks to work out, ya know what i mean? but like, do you want to talk about this wife of yours?

Harrison says:

Not really, no. She's a bitch. She's been taping our phone conversations, Jason. She played one to her lawyer, and I was cursing because she didn't bring our son for his visit for the third time. But wouldn't you curse, Jason?

Jason is typing…

Harrison says:

She tries to make me curse. She instigates. Makes me look bad.

Jason says:

yeah, i would curse. most def. oh, that's messed up. but now you have nogo, right? so it's all good.

Harrison says:

No! Thank you for reminding me. It's not all good. I just want to, ok, so what you're telling me is that there's no way to turn off the premium filters? How about turning the whole program off?

Jason says:

it will automatically go off when your contract is up

Harrison says:

But I only need it when corresponding with my ox-wifo or my lawyor. I havo work o-mailc to cond. It's too slow.

Jason says:

what kind of music do you listen to?

Harrison says:

Music?

Jason says:

yeah. i'm supposed to ask personal questions. good customer service or whatever.

Harrison says:

I like, god I guess I haven't been listening to much music. I...you seem like a nice kid, Jason, but please take pity on an old man. How do I work this thing?

Jason says:

try typing the e-mail in word and then copy/pasting it. all the filters will appear afterwards anyway i bet, but at least you can get your thoughts out maybe

Harrison says:

Oh, you're a genius, Jason! Thank you!

Jason says:

no prob, dude. listen, check out some bad religion if you haven't. they're old skool but amazing. "This is not entertainment," you know what I mean? "Maintain against the grain."

Harrison says:

Sure thing, Jason. Thanks

New

Document 13

Dear Sandy,

Look, I'm going to level with you. The way you're handling [Psychoanalytic Filter has something to Say.] [Psycho-analytic Filter has been ignored.] fuck! The way you're manipulating [Basic Service suggests replacing the word manipulating. Suggested replacements include: manag-ing, directing, controlling.] [Are you sure you want to ignore Basic Service?] [Basic service has been ignored.] God. What do I even do? [Literary Genius has something to say.] [Literary Genius has been ignored.] IGNORE!!! Shove it literature!

Are you sure you want to: Erase all Nogo© comments?

Nogo© comments have been successfully erased ✓

Dear Sandy,

Look, I'm going to level with you. The way you're handling fuck! The way you're manipulating God. What do I even do? IGNORE!!! Shove it literature!

Love,

Harrison

-christ.

Harrison says:

Hello? Nogo? Jason?

Beverly says:

Hello, Mr. Brooks. Seabird in your gullet?

Harrison says:

What!? I want to talk to Jason, please.

Beverly says:

Jason got fired. Right after chatting with you. Nothing ventured nothing gained.

Harrison says:

Oh man. He was a good kid. Why didn't they fire you? Can I talk to a manager then, Beverly? This is ridiculous. I can't even use Microsoft Word without being interrupted by this stupid software.

Beverly says:

Glad you asked, Harrison. We'd have to get up pretty early in the morning to get one by you, wouldn't we? Hang on. It'll be just a minute. Take deep breaths. The whole universe is inside you.

Harrison says:

Yeah, thanks for that, Bev. Really.

-sleep
-frightened
-truck
-thief

-this
-is
-kind
-of
-fun
-words:
-flashlight
-brasserie
-remember?
-paris?
-waiting
-WAITING
-beanpole
-ciggarettes
-culpable
-palpate
-willow-wine-barrister.   Oh-look-a-dash-works-laterally!-
the-latitude-of-stolen-children-you-are-stealing-my-child-
sandy!-dear-sandy-honestly-I-stuck-the-fork-in-the-door-
-for-a-reason-I-thought-blood-tests-i-thought-why'd-you-
cheat-on-me-
territory-club-fist.
-dick
-bag
-that
-friggin
-guy
-last-week-mikey-he-said-he-told-some-kid-he-wished-
he'd-be-deceased-out-loud-he-said-"i-wish-you'd-be-
deceased!"-but-he-didn't-punch-the-bully-he-put-the-

spoon-down-and-looked-at-me-testing-i-remember-you-
said-you-didn't-want-to-bring-a-child-into-the-world-you-
said-three-million-orphans-in-iraq-you-said-you-put-the-
paper-down-you-said-twenty-years-until-the-place-is-
too-hot-you-thought-fire-we'd-become-fire-we-did-you-
said-but-we-did-and-no-offence-but-i-don't-care-about-
you-anymore-still-i-never-knew-I'd-remember-morning-
banana-smells-and-that-restaurant-we-found-in-paris-
with-the-mosaic-table-and-we-saw-letters-on-a-piece-
of-glass-and-made-up-meanings-in-english-j.-m.-c.-and-
you-said-jelly-meets-curtains-and-i-said-jiggle-my-cock-
and-you-laughed-and-hit-my-arm-and-i-don't-care-about-
you-but-i-do-remember-and-i-just-miss-him-my-son-and-
you-lied-you-said

-I've
-forgotten.

-look
-at
-that.

-oh
-yeah
-yes-you-said.
-yes
-and
-you
-said
-even

-steven
-half
-time
-fifty
-fifty
-visits
-are
-monthly
-now-and-when-you-do-bring-him-you're-late-and-when-
i-show-up-you're-not-there-and-i-wanted-him-my-son-I-
always-did-from-the-beginning.

-i-bought-him-a-ferry-boat
-one
-two
-three
-where-can-you-be-oh-sand-eee?
-in-a-vacumed-explorer-with-held-hand-in-cupholder-
and-bucket-seat-cherry-leather?

-little
-league
-fuck.

-I-can't-breathe-they-say-xanax-but-I-think-it's-asthma-
and-they-don't-believe-me-and-the-courts-favor-the-
mother-even-when-she-leaves-and-unsnaps-her-dress-
for-a-mustached-man-in-her-husband's-hallway-you-
know-i-paid-for-that-fucking-hallway-while-you-went-to-
school-I-memo'd-people-blue-for-that-hallway-that-was-

my-hallway.
-he
-was
-right
-there
-mikey
-my
-son
-right
-down
-my
-hallway
-when
-you
-did
-this
-did-he-tell-you-he-wants-to-make-someone-deceased?

Bart James says:

Mr. Brooks?

Harrison says:

Yes! Hello? I'm a new Nogo customer and I

Bart James says:

Oh, yes. I know exactly who you are.

Harrison says:

don't like it.

Bart James is typing…

Bart James says:

I've been following you on live edit for some time and I just looked through your chat history. Your son wants to make someone deceased, huh?

Harrison says:

That's weird. I, you could see that? I thought the dash warded you off or something.

Bart James says:

Well it scrambles the efficiency of the automated editors. Goodness knows why you'd want to do that! ☺ You certainly need them...

Harrison says:

I was just, I got carried away, I guess—pent up energy—in the middle of a custody battle—point is I want to remove the Nogo service. I'm ... unsatisfied.

Bart James says:

You signed an agreement, sir. And in a time like this you wouldn't want your violent history unoarthed.

Harrison says:

Violent history? What are you talking about? Look, it's not the money

Bart James says:

"I wouldn't mind getting rid of my wife" "she's a bitch" ??? ☺

Harrison says:

That's taken out of context! Jesus Christ!

Bart James says:

Exactly, Mr. Brooks. That's exactly what these lawyers do—take things out of context. We're here to protect you from all that <3

Harrison says:

It doesn't sound like that's what you're here to do. It sounds like bribery, to mention something like that.

Bart James says:

We have no reason to bribe you Mr. Brooks, but it's exactly these kinds of accusations that paint a picture of a certain character. If you know what I mean

Harrison says:

There you go again!

Bart James says:

You signed an agreement, sir. Do you not read the agreements you sign?

Harrison says:

Who reads agreements?

Bart James says:

I do, sir. I read them.

Harrison says:

I'll be speaking with my Lawyer about this.

Bart James says:

As you wish, Sir

Compose Message:

Greg,

I tried calling you five times and now I'm just WRITING THIS ON NOGO BECAUSE I HAVE NOTHING TO HIDE!!! **[Psychoanalytic Filter has something to Say.] [Psychoanalytic Filter has been ignored.]** This company you recommended is spying **[Basic Service suggests replacing the word: spying. Suggested replacements include: looking, noticing, gazing.] [Basic Service has been ignored.]** fine! HARASSING **[Basic Service suggests replacing the word: ~~HARASSING~~. Suggested replacements include: nudging, teasing, tickling.] [Basic Service has been ignored.]** Tickling? my ass! **[Psychoanalytic Filter has something to Say.] [Psychoanalytic Filter has been ignored.]** $@%^@$%^@#$%!#@$%$#!% Houston we have a problem-don't tell me to call it a snag or a conundrum, computer, because it is a PROBLEM-don't interrupt when I'm sending out an S.O.S-message in a bottle. **[Psychoanalytic Filter has something to Say.] [Psychoanalytic Filter has been ignored.]** i-bottle?-oh-because-it's-shaped-like-a-dick?-good-lord-nogo-i-guess-i-have-to-type-in-dash-

es-like-a-nut-job-to-beat-this-thing-but-greg-please-help-
me-this-is-crazy-I'm-being-silenced

-Harrison

Your message has been sent. View message

Silenced-dum-de-dum-dum-dum. Dumb-ditty-ditty-dumb-
dumb. Ba-doot-doot-dah-doot-doot-ditty-ditty-NOTHING!-
oh-nothing, NOGO, da-da-dee-da-dee-doty-la-la-la-la-la-
bamba-ah-nececito-huevos-whirlygigs-getdown-
Whistle-while-you-wait-dah-da-dat-dat-dat-doot-doot-

GREGORY!

show details 4:07 PM (0 minutes ago)

Dear Harrison,

**"JUST WRITING THIS ON NOGO BECAUSE I HAVE
NOTHING TO HIDE!!! This company you recommended is spying fine! HARASSING Tickling? my ass!—
$@%^@$%^@#$%!#@$%$#!% Houston we have a
problem-don't tell me to call it a snag or a conundrum,
computer, because it is a PROBLEM-don't interrupt
when I'm sending out an S.O.S-message in a bottle
-i-bottle?-oh-because-it's-shaped-like-a-dick?-good-
lord-nogo-i-guess-i-have-to-type-in-dashes-like-a-
nut-job-to-beat-this-thing-but-greg-please-help-me-
this-is-crazy-I'm-being-silenced-Harrison"**

I have no idea what to make of the above statement. That
it came through email is just ... please be patient in the
future. Have I ever not returned your voicemails?

As your lawyer I'm worried about you. I know custody battles can be stressful, but I don't want it to jeopardize the progression of the case. Time is money, you know? I made you an appointment with a psychologist. Dr. Beverly Sisterne. She was the only one I found who could see you right away, she retired from private practice but was willing to make an exception. I've worked with her in the past. She has excellent qualifications and specializes in stress management. This evening at 6:00, 123 Lincoln at Waterbeard, Suite B. Please go, Harry. I know you love your son, and I know we can win this, but you've got to keep it together. I don't want this to take years. For your sake.

Best,

Greg

P.S. — To be cont.

ascent

no, go,
continued

Beverly says:

I feel our session tonight really helped you. You seem to understand now.

Harrison says:

Mmm hmm.

Beverly says:

Picturing your happy place Is tried and true.

Harrison says:

Oh yes.

Beverly says:

Anger is toxic.

Harrison says:

All I feel is happiness, Beverly. I'm like a bird.

Beverly says:

Have you tried writing your wife? No man is an island.

Harrison says:

What a good idea, Beverly.

Compose Message:

Dear Sandy,

I believe this will work out for the best for all concerned. I appreciate your patience as we work toward a compromise regarding custody. Family must sometimes take on new shapes, our roles are simply being redefined. It is natural that we meet challenges along the way. I am confident that we will both meet the present needs of the situation.

Best regards,

Harrison

Your message has been sent. View message

Beverly is typing...

Beverly says:

Your case is looking up, Harrison.

Harrison says:

Whatever it takes or how my heart breaks.

Beverly says:

...I will be RIGHT here WAITING for you... love that song, sigh...

Harrison says:

I thought you might.

Beverly says:

Oh that was fast! I see that your conversation has been updated.

Harrison says:

The conversation is always being updated, right Bev?

Beverly says:

Oh yes. But I meant literally—there's a new message from Sandy in your inbox.

Harrison says:

Thank you Beverly. I'll have a look-see.

show details 11:08 PM (0 minutes ago)

Dear Harrison,

What in God's religion? Big Bird's this is not my unconscious you stupid name? is this load of excrement? Do you remember what you called me when you last at the end of time there may be a convergence of roads undone returned I'm not a freakin poet literary genius! Covered in dew fuck! Picked up your child kid son Mikey Jesus! not as if—You are a prick pin needle. Copulation with you put things in its mouth and pulled with its tongue gums? Like what jesus! As if with a lollipop. Do you know what I comprehend my undercurrent? You confronted my boyfriend in the nose! You lied misspoke lies untruth about me in the ears of my child kid son Mikey Jesus! FOR THE LOVE OF A MONOTHEISTIC FORCE!!! You told him I was a wanton strumpet! But not that your member could not become erect without shiny sighing body parts shaved on simulated camera shows or that you worked so many hours and never said words that would make my lungs open and heart fuck commas! New shapes? I'll give you new shapes right in your nether region you offspring of a female dog! Because the world is a fragment split of unkind death soul damn! And I was scared mildly put off when fertilized but what right do you contain to challenge my authority as a mother GOD! I told him to confront that bully misunderstood youth right in the nose like you should have you darned hippy hypocrite swaying in the wind on a hill with music notes for eyes. IGNORE LITERARY GENIUS!

I will see you in court you anus indenture.

Signed,

Sandy

Beverly says:

I recommend activating auto reply, Harrison.

Harrison says:

Yes. Auto reply has been successfully downloaded, thank you.

Autoreply has been successfully downloaded ✓

B   u   t,
M.I.K.E.Y?
                              In
C)a)s)e
W
e\are/separated-   Bever

                                                    Bever

                                                    Is this
                                                    desig
                                                    Nogo
                                                    snag

know this:

i.a.m.a.w.e.e.d.m.i.k.e.y.a.n.d.s.o.a.r.e.y.o.u...
.w.i.l.d.n.o.c.o.n.c.rect

can   Harri

                                                    Artwo
                                                    hobb
                                                    of mi

stop----------us   Bever

                                                    Is it s
                                                    progr

Harri

no,b,u,l,l,y,no,m,o,m,no,go,

Don't

no, go,   never

jeapo

win th

case

iwould

Bever

n

e   I sup

ver   go   never   resul

healin

L***E***A***V***E

You.   Harri

Will(not)go(lightly)but(just)in(case)i(have)to(go)   Exact

Activate Auto Reply?

Autoreply has been successfully activated ✓

words Mikey-

Dear Sandy,

Thank you for your prompt response. I am always happy to
receive your feedback.

Best,

Harrison

Mikey-If-you-get-sad-you-can-say-truck-thief-you-can-say-pollywog-any-word!

Piston-or-top hat or gloss cereal popsicle or even

(Shit)

Approve Auto Reply's message?

Auto Reply's message has been approved ✓

d&o&n&t&l&e&t&t&h&e&m&t&a&k&e&y&o&u&r&w&o&r
&d&s&m&y&son

ferret-stool-gradient-belligerent-talisman-assunder-thunder-bones-honey-wind-tapestry-and-ass

they   are   yours.

I
Hope
You
Will
You
Will
You
Will@see@this@note@some@day@love@d@a@d.

Your message has been sent. View message

(clearing)

not the problem

Granddaughter places Grandmother in a good spot, shady but with sun streaks. She kisses her head and leaves her there, but does not forget to bring food. "This is the problem," she says, about the grandmother just sitting there. Out in the open. In her spot. She brings crossword puzzles and kisses to the grandmother also, but it is still the problem. She buys fancy purses and runs around with young men so as to change the subject.

The grandmother becomes particularly interested in a family of spiders. Spiders are usually lone creatures, just they and their spindlies and whatever they catch. But nope, not these, they are a family. Mama Spider, Papa Spider, Baby Spider, Middle Child Spider, and Oldest Child Spider.

The web is spectacular with overlays of silver upon silver. The children dye their corners of the web in putrid colors to express their individuality, but the web gets wind blown and trampled often. This provides Mother Spider with redecorating excuses. The grandmother marvels at this web making, the beautiful tendrils. How each strand shines. Each family member has particular threads they travel upon in each new web. Their feet like accordions, their bodies strew their own patterns atop their mother's.

Baby Spider prefers black and likes to torture his prey for an inordinate amount of time, citing despair as a condition of existence. The grandmother can't hear *exactly* what he says, but she can intuit it. "Ah the futility of it all!" she hears. "The certain death!" He asks her questions like, "What would I be if I could no longer make silk?" She picks him up and holds him when he prattles like this. She feels sorry for him.

Mother Spider did not at first appreciate this behavior. She bit the grandmother's foot and it itched for a week and left a mark. Now she's gotten used to it. She even climbs atop the grandmother's finger herself when Papa Spider has disappeared again. The grandmother can see where Papa Spider goes. It's a shame, she says and shakes her head. But she doesn't give the mother the details. She doesn't want her webs to come out less delicately enameled, or for her to stop visiting her fingertip.

Her granddaughter's visits become more and more of a nuisance. She's knocked into the web twice. When the grandmother tries to tell her about the intricate sensitivities of Middle Spider, the granddaughter only half listens and then checks her head for a fever. Besides, her guilt is annoying. "This is not the problem," says the grandmother. But she is not heard.

Oldest Spider hears her though. Oldest Spider refuses to believe in problems. Oldest Spider runs around reciting mantras of success to himself and shares them with the grandmother. "A problem is only an opportunity in disguise/You have to visualize the future you want." Oldest Spider trails after his father and also knows where he goes, and atop Grandmother's finger, he will sometimes crack and shed a few tiny gossamer tears. Grandmother loves these moments. She feels she is helping.

Grandmother recalls Charlotte's Web and asks Mother Spider one day if her time is almost up. The grandmother does not want to wind up a sad pig. Or even a radiant one. Mother Spider laughs at her. "I'll outlive you, you old bag. That's for sure." This is her sense of humor. The grandmother laughs and laughs and wets herself a little. Her granddaughter brings her disposable undies all the while muttering her guilt.

Grandmother does not appreciate that all the spiders will know she wet herself, but she gets over it. She knows, for example, that Middle Child Spider sneaks her boyfriend into her part of the web at night. She knows what they do! Once she would have been appalled by Middle Spider's morals, but she's loosened up in her old age. You can't control the young. Or much of anything for that matter. Middle Spider occasionally bites Grandmother too, and also bites her own arms. She is tired of living in her mother's web. She feels her legs are not slender enough and that her face is not pretty and so forth. Spiders differentiate between arms and legs. This is all very interesting to the unsuspecting grandmother.

The grandmother does not understand where Middle Spider gets this. Spiders do not read fashion magazines or celebrity gossip. They do not watch MTV, unless they are trapped in the house of a human teenager. But even then there are seldom any spiders on MTV. She thinks of her granddaughter and inadvertently gulps. She reassures Middle that she is a lovely spider, just lovely. (Really the grandmother can't tell the difference.) This is when Middle Spider bites her. She can't understand *exactly* what Grandmother is saying, but she knows a lie when she feels one. There is no talking to Middle Spider sometimes. In these instances the grandmother will admit that she is a human and an old one. "I don't understand about spider teenagers," she'll say. "I just think you are a dear and that's the truth. And that boyfriend of yours doesn't know what he's missing out on." (The boyfriend had recently stopped coming around. Why buy the cow, if you know what I mean.) To this the middle child spider would weep and weep until the grandmother's finger was soaked and then she'd apologize and wind her silks around Grandmother's finger to dry it. This delighted her. She felt included. Also, it tickled.

The grandmother soon took to imitating the spiders. She dug up her old yarn and attempted to weave webs of string. She felt surrounded by colorful spaghetti, but not a web. She even tucked the yarn between her legs and walked slowly around releasing string from her bottom. The spiders snickered at her broken mandala nest and so did Grandmother. Her foot had begun to bother her, though, so she stopped trying to perfect her new craft.

Her foot was disturbing her actually. When her granddaughter came around she would hide it under a pillow. What was disturbing about her foot was that there was a hole in it.

Each day the hole seemed to grow. It began like a dime, then it was a nickel, then a quarter, then a silver dollar, and now she avoided the topic.

Mother Spider asked to look at the wound. She'd spied limping. She began to weep when she saw it, which made Grandmother even more nervous. Nervous Nellie. She played solitaire to relax. She said to herself: old age is weird. All sorts of strange things happen in old age. But then a hole began to grow on her hand, too. Terrible, the grandmother thought. But busied herself cooking up schemes that would make Middle Spider's boyfriend jealous, or give Baby Spider a dose of optimism (just enough), or allow Oldest Spider to be more honest and forgiving with himself.

The family was acting strange with her, she noticed. Perhaps it was the stench? The grandmother had begun to smell. She felt awfully embarrassed about it. She bathed herself with baby wipes, but to no avail. Worse, it seemed that every time she struck up a conversation with one of the spiders they began to weep. Even Papa Spider, who wasn't much of a cryer. And when she accidentally bumped their web, they rebuilt it farther away from her chair. They'd never done that before! She could hardly hear their conversations now. It stunk worse than she did, quite frankly.

The granddaughter came on a Tuesday. The pillow was over the foot, and the hand was stuffed into a spool of yarn. Air freshener had been spurted. Perfume had been spritzed. The grandmother concocted a most innocent face. The granddaughter clicked around in her heels murmuring. She knew something was up.

"Why is your hand stuffed in a spool of yarn?" she asked.

"It's like a fancy baseball mitt, isn't it?" the grandmother replied innocently. The eyebrows shot up. Oh brother she thought. "I just like the way it feels. Warm." Eyebrow release. Close one. The grandmother hated hospitals. She hated them very much.

"Grandma, it smells weird."

"New air freshener," she said and swatted her mitt in dismissal. The yarn spool slid off a little. She hurried to secure it and in her flabbergasted state she stood up. The pillow slipped from her foot.

The granddaughter vomited on the ground when she saw the hole. It was the size and color of a hamburger patty. She barely missed baby spider with her throw up. He leapt out of the way just in time and blinked all of his eyes, gasping.

"Ohmygodohmygodohmygod!!!" the granddaughter said.

"No hospitals. Please!? No hospitals," said the grandmother.

"I'm sorry Grandma, but you have to go. That's disgusting! What *happened* to you?"

"I don't know! I hate the hospital! Can I go see Dr. Rob?"

"NO! He won't have the equipment for something like this. Stay here I'm going to pull my car up." The granddaughter left, shaking her wrists and cursing.

The grandmother returned from the hospital a week later without a finger, but the doctors were able to save most of the hand and the foot with up-to-date packing materials. The spider family stared at her. All five of them in a row. The grandmother stared right back.

"You're supposed to be reclusive!" the grandmother shouted.

"I know," Mother Spider said with shiny eyes. But no tears slipped out. "We were trying something different," she said.

"Oh, like biting old women who are supposed to be your friend!" The grandmother turned her head and jutted out her chin to show the family that she was inconsolable.

"We have no control over the poison! Please believe us!" Middle Spider said. But the grandmother started humming and held her dramatic chin position.

"Lets look on the bright side," said Oldest Spider, true to form. "You didn't die, and you didn't lose the foot." He attempted a smile. The grandmother glared at him. It was progress.

"I had to spend a whole week with a dying woman who smelled even worse than me! I probably caught a terminal illness!" retorted the grandmother. "And I'm missing a finger!"

Baby Spider said, "I for one never bit you." The grandmother nodded but then repositioned her chin.

Middle Spider said desperately, "I think you're a dear, and that's the truth."

"Come here, you little wench!" The grandmother said. "You see how it feels!" She'd had enough. She picked up Middle Spider and brought her to her mouth. Middle Spider started screaming and so did Mother Spider. Baby Spider was cracking up laughing. The father and Oldest Spider paced. The grandmother swallowed Middle Spider without crunching down and then burst into tears. Middle Spider had been her favorite, the little hussy. The rest of the family crawled up her legs and began biting with abandon, except for Baby Spider, who just watched. Grandmother didn't even fight it. She would become an old piece of Jarlsburg. It was better than cancer. She would finally be rid of that annoying granddaughter. Perhaps there was an afterlife. Maybe she'd see her husband again, or at least her cat. Not that she deserved it. She began to drift off. But then she felt a biting sensation in her esophagus.

Middle spider was still alive!

"Middle spider?" the grandmother said as if putting her ear to a closed bedroom door.

"sdjkhfa anwupfhuawlfkjh!!!" was all she heard.

"Mother Spider, she's alive!" the grandmother said. "Come here!" She plucked Mother Spider from the place where she'd been biting and brought her to her chest. Mother Spider conversed with her daughter through the grandmother's skin and ribcage. The grandmother tried not to overhear, but no she didn't try.

"She's drowning!" said Mother Spider. "I can barely understand her!"

"Tell her she must find someplace dry!" said the grandmother. "Heart," she thought.

"I'm going in after her," the mother announced. She stuck the end of her silk to one of Grandmother's molars and descended into her throat. The father and Oldest Spider moved up to the grandmother's chest and tried to hear what was going on over the thunderous heartbeat. The grandmother didn't close her mouth. Her attempted murder had erased her anger. She was going to die anyway. But maybe she could save her friend. She just let the drool pool and spill and held her head back.

"Oh for the love of God!" the granddaughter said, wielding a can of Riddance. She just shows up like that sometimes, it's terrible. She started spraying right at Grandmother. Grandmother cupped her wet hand around the boys.

"Why is your mouth hanging open?" the granddaughter asked.

"I ono," the grandmother said without closing her mouth.

"What do you mean you don't know?"

"I ono!!"

"Does anything hurt?" She patted her grandmother down and checked for fever. Thank goodness she was wearing a long skirt to hide the fresh bites. It was a terrible moment for Mother Spider to emerge from the grandmother's throat triumphantly wielding her daughter. But this was the moment that it happened. It was nearly impossible not to cough, but the grandmother was strong. Her face turned red.

"Eh, Eh!" the grandmother warned. If they stayed in her mouth the granddaughter might miss them. She felt them crawling over her tongue. They didn't know what "Eh, Eh!" had meant. The grandmother gently closed her lips leaving a hollow in her mouth. This understandably freaked the spiders out. They would start biting in moments, she knew. She waved her granddaughter away.

"I'm not leaving until I know you're safe!" the granddaughter said.

The grandmother kicked a nearby bucket to create a distraction and in the instant that her granddaughter turned her head, she coughed Mother and Middle Spider and a big puddle of drool into her right hand. Her left hand was still cupping Father and Oldest Spider to her chest. God knows where Baby Spider was, likely spinning silks in her wounds like Sisyphus again. The doctors had found the soft remains of his previous attempts.

Her granddaughter turned back to her and put her hands on her hips. This didn't even annoy the grandmother because she was so happy her plan had worked and she was even more happy to be able to swallow again. She swallowed and swallowed and swallowed and smiled. She cupped her two hands together to reunite the family. The cup had a hole in it where her pointer finger was missing.

"What is the matter with you?" the granddaughter asked.

"Nothing. I'm fine. What is the matter with you?"

"Me? Nothing I'm fine."

"Fine. We're all fine here. Are you done spraying? Because I was about to take a nap." She yawned.

The granddaughter thought a nap was a fine idea. Healthy. Something had been up, but all seemed well now. She sighed.

"Oh, alright. I guess you must be tired." She said this in a poor baby voice, which revolted the grandmother, but the revulsion stirred itself quickly into pity for the young woman's problem.

"Oh yes," the grandmother said and stretched. The granddaughter turned, reluctant to leave. She looked back and said I love you and Grandmother winked at her. She loved her too, even if she was annoying.

When Grandmother heard the ignition she opened her hands. The spiders sprinkled out. They were moving all slow.

"What's the matter?" Grandmother asked.

"My legs hurt and my eyes are burning," Oldest Spider said. The others mumbled agreement.

"The Riddance!" Grandmother said. She started to cry. What a shame that after everything they would die anyway. She hadn't realized it would be powerful enough to get past her hands. "We're all going to die!" the grandmother said.

"Told you," said a voice in her eardrum. Baby Spider!

"Where are you!?" said Grandmother. "You missed every-thing!"

"No I didn't, I'm right here."

"I don't see you."

"In your ear."

"My ear?! Hahaha, it tickles."

"It didn't tickle until you knew I was here."

"Hahaha!"

The rest of the family lay dazed on her shirt. They looked up at the sound of their son/brother's voice. They seemed to understand something. The grandmother didn't feel so well either. Her face was burning and she was shivering. Time to go, that's all. At least she wasn't alone in some horrible hospital. But what about Baby?

"What will you do when we're all gone?" she asked him.

"I will go on," he said. "Trap flies and avoid birds."

"How will you escape the Riddance?" Grandmother asked. She was getting sleepy.

"I'll stay in your ear for awhile, I suppose."

"Oh that's nice," Grandmother said. "That's very nice." But she was only half listening. Baby Spider hummed.

two angels

I'm thinking I'm about to level up here at Berryman Consultants, because you should see my screen when I log in. I have 459 approvals, 35 helpouts, 4 honesties, and an angel. I do also have 6 crabapples, but everybody has bad days. In case you're wondering about the honesties, they are hard to get on our app, because when you click on an honesty you have to answer all of these questions about the incident and people are lazy, you know? That was crabapple. I'm giving myself a crabapple because who cares? With this many approvals and helpouts? I can be *honest* about my crabapples. I wish I could give myself an honesty too. I can give myself an approval but it looks bad. Like bragging—which is kind of crabapple. You can get in a real loop with the ratings.

In case you are wondering about my honesties—I *confessed* when I was *overpaid*. I mean, who does that? I won't tell you about the others.

This is a great job, though. I mean, it doesn't pay so well. And we've all given our CEO a crabapple for this at least once. He's a sport about crabapples, though. But the point is we feel appreciated. Some people in some companies don't bother giving out helpouts or even approvals, which literally take one second. I used to just keep the app out on my phone, because I discovered that you have to be generous to secure a lot of clicks. It isn't just that I handed out approvals like donuts, though, I mean, I really earned my helpouts and my honesties are second to none. I think I'm the first employee in the history of the company to get four. We only started the system last year, but still. It really works. You should see the smiles when people log in. Sure, some people are less popular, but that would be true in any system. It serves as a stand in for the evolutionary fact that some people shouldn't work with you. Whiney people should start their own company where they give each other whineys all day. That was a joke.

We don't have a whiney button. We do have a failure button. Not everyone is allowed to use it, but I can because of my helpout level. I failed Smith Birthright—who has a name like that? He deserves another failure for his name. I failed him every time he passed my desk because I didn't like his smell. I, like, *hated* his smell. It wasn't that he was dirty I don't think, it was some kind of terrible cologne mixed with I don't know, ass sweat and baby powder? God. I'm relieved to report he got fired. I bet you're also wondering about my angel. Emoji with tongue out. It wouldn't be smart of me to tell you how I earned an angel, would it? I mean angels are the hardest of all. I had to go to HR for a drug test before it would even show up on my screen. Not that they suspected me, it's just procedure for angels. All the admins were in a fluster because angels are so rare that they all forgot what they were supposed to do. They had to dig out some folder for directions. The last person to get an angel was our CEO and guess how many he has? One. Same as me. Glowing emoji. We're on a first name basis and not because of how I earned my angel. It's more of a respect thing. Even though I still work in a cubicle. Google eyes.

Marybeth brought me coffee. She's not an assistant, she's just trying to get an approval. What happens when you've gathered as many positives as I have is that your approvals increase their worth. I click once and someone gets five approvals. So I'm basically like royalty around here at this point. Every time I open my screen I have more approvals because people are fishing for mine. I've had to become more conservative with my clicks lately. Don't want the finger to hurt at the end of the day. Smiley. You don't want to feel desperate is what it is. Like if you follow more people than follow you. But you have to throw people a bone click once and awhile to keep theirs coming in. I opened my screen. 467 and another helpout—and I didn't even do anything! I love my work.

Clients can give us approvals too, but they hardly ever do. It's not that they aren't satisfied. We keep trying to explain this to our CEO. It's like how checkout counters give you surveys with your receipt sometimes, and they're like, if you fill this out we enter you in a sweepstakes for a laptop. Even if you want a laptop, you don't fill it out. You throw the receipt in the bag and forget about that laptop. In this analogy we are the laptop, I told our CEO. Or the receipt? He looked at me strangely. He's been looking at me strangely lately. The point is that people are busy and they want to get home to a bowl of pasta and Jeopardy so unfortunately even if we're unforgettable we're forgettable.

Ever since the angel our CEO has been looking at me like an emoji with its eyebrows raised. I suggested at our last meeting that our satisfaction screens pop up for clients *before* checkout. So that they think they *have* to approve us or they won't complete their purchase. That made our CEO's eyebrows go down. He called me brilliant in that staff meeting, which was three days ago. At this point I'm still waiting for a positivity to show up on my screen. His clicks are worth the most amount of approvals. A helpout, even, is in order, I would think. I'm a little sad about it to be honest. Open screen. 489! Just for sitting here! But nothing that confirms I'm brilliant. I'm considering giving him a crabapple. I really am.

Instead I give him an approval, the fourth approval since that meeting. He doesn't get the hint, I don't think, that he's being an ass.

Omg, he walked by and tapped my desk! What does that mean? He hardly ever comes out here. Still nothing on the screen. 494. Maybe I should march right into his office and earn another angel. It wouldn't look good, though. People might talk. Like last time. All those weird giggles. But who cares? My approvals would be worth so much with another angel, they'd be buying me sushi lunches instead of bagels and coffee. Yum, sushi lunches. I looked in the mirror and it was like I could see the halo. Now I have Beyoncé in my head. Google.

I did it. I marched in there. No angel at this point, but these things take time. This angel should be quicker because HR already has a file for me. But something weird is going on, currently. Marybeth and Johnson looked at me and giggled when I went to the bathroom. When I got back I checked my screen and I almost had a heart attack. Everything was at zero. My approvals, helpouts, honesties, angel, and even crabapples were all at zero. So I went back into our CEO's office and told him there had been some sort of a mistake. He said there must have been a glitch in the app and waved me away because he got a phone call. I went to IT and they were all busy checking their screens and their screens were *not* at zero. They giggled at me too. They said they'd get right on it and I said hurry up please and when I got back to my desk I had four crabapples. I'm really beside myself, here! Four crabapples and no approvals is grounds for a demotion and sure enough, I have an email from HR asking me to make an appointment. Maybe it's for my angel. Maybe they've been notified of the glitch and have the correct numbers in their files.

But no, I went and talked to HR and it was a disaster! They didn't know anything about the second angel or my correct numbers. I explained that they could trust me that I was at 492 with approvals and 36 with helpouts. I gave myself an extra of the latter for the idea I had at the meeting, because someone had to. They said they didn't know what to tell me, they had no record, which is bullshit, because Marybeth is in HR, and why did she buy me coffee, then? She bought me coffee because she knew how much my approvals were worth because of my numbers. But I didn't say that because I didn't want more crabapples. I just calmly said, "Come on guys, you can trust me. I have four honesties!" They turned their faces to my screen of zeros they'd pulled up, and then looked up at me and shrugged. They shook their heads and gave me I'm so sorry but really I'm not eyes. Marybeth said, "I just don't see any honesties here." I took a deep breath to stop myself from a full throttle conniption and left the room.

12 Crabapples.

Pete Hartman asked me if I want to get a drink after work. Pete Hartman! His skin is practically translucent and you can see his veins. He's been here for ten years and only has three approvals. Pity approvals. Shove it, Hartman, I wanted to tell him. But I looked at my screen. I had three approvals too. From Hartman. I looked up at him with an emoji that doesn't exist yet.

I went to have the drink with Hartman. Man it was tough to keep the conversation going. He's one of those types who forgets he's in a social situation and sinks into himself. His eyes go all vacant and his bags sag. I would fish him out and then, plunk. He'd submerge back down into the river of pale guys, or wherever he goes. At some point, I had him on the line because I asked him about Comic Con and I managed to steer the conversation into Berryman stuff. Speaking of mutants, I said, and then I had to ask him why everyone seemed to hate me all of the sudden real quick before his eyes glazed.

They think you're giving him blowjobs, was Hartman's answer.

As if he were saying can I buy another round, which he would never say, because he's cheap and doesn't understand how to get approvals on or off screen.

What?

The only person who has the power to delete your contents, though is Sam.

Sam, our CEO. Haloface.

So your approvals problem must be with him. The blow-job theories are causing the giggles around the office, though.

I stared at Hartman for a full three seconds.

Then I slapped him.

In the face.

Hard.

I know I shouldn't have slapped the messenger, but I hauled off and did. I fully slapped the messenger. Right in his face.

I was immediately glad I did.

His white face turned pink as a piglet. His eyes spilled the tears of the pale guy river.

Listen you little punk, I said, I DID NOT give SAM a BLOWJOB.

He spattered incoherently, but some words bubbled up and popped, and I discerned that Hartman was only out with me because he thought maybe he could get a blowjob too.

I stood up, because you know when anger switches intensity and becomes so strong you become extremely calm? Basically at that point you can burn a hole in a soul or a stomach lining through your eyeholes. I brought my mouth up to Hartman's droopy face and spoke directly into it. I told him all about his shriveled little alabaster dick and precisely where he could stick it, which is nowhere, ever. I also said some things that were maybe mean. Highlights possibly include some negative inferences about his mother, and how he would die alone picking scabs off of his ashen, prostitute-addled tongue, because the best he could hope for was that a crackhead might one day relent and let him suck her off for her fix. I said this all in a low and focused voice, almost a whisper, until he collapsed from his bar stool and sobbed in my arms. Good. There, there, my Tiny Lonesome. There, there.

Then we were able to have a humane conversation.

First it involved pathetic confessions from Hartman, which I endured, waiting for the opportunity to clear my good name. There was some crap about high school, something about people spitting on him? I don't know. I wasn't really listening. I was staring up at the propensity for vodka flavors to propagate. Whipped cream? Bubblegum? When he'd finished, and the bar patrons had politely cleared a space around us and made their way to the green lit cocktail tables, I peeled his slick face from my collarbone and sat him down.

Now, Hartman is a squirmy-worm, but he isn't dumb. He was the odd bird who survived the aura of general distaste his presence spawned because he had a brain. So he was valuable to the company, unfortunately. I pressed him.

Why does Sam have a problem with me?

I don't know! I thought he had a problem with you because he was uncomfortable with the sex acts!

He whined and wheezed, sighing. He was in the vulnerable stage of spent. I pressed harder. I pinched.

I need you to listen to me, Hartman, I said. I did not give Sam sex acts, okay? I donated my monthly commissions to his foundation.

The one he started for women with failing boob jobs?

Yes. The one his mother made him start when her lefty burst. The one that helps him avoid taxes while other wealthy tax evaders also avoid medical bills.

The one that has the webpage with the pink ribbon?

Yes, the one that gives a single percent of its philanthropic mission to breast cancer research and donations to survivors that need augmentation following surgery, while the rest of the money goes to cosmetic improvements for women who spend more on a handbag than I do on rent.

The one that he asks us to donate some of our bonus to when he gets us drunk enough at Christmas parties, and we do, because he paints pictures of an apocalyptic world with deteriorating racks littering the cityscape?

Yeah, that one.

You should have just sucked his cock, Hartman said.

He punctuated his comment with a sip from his cherry pie vodka, like he simply didn't give a single fuck anymore.

I laughed. He was right. It was pretty much the same. I sucked our CEO's mother's lefty, basically. It was less direct. It was only one percent better.

I looked into Hartman's sunken blues and saw a plastic baby pool of something more there than I'd detected before. I could also see that he had the feeling that our work here was done. We'd thoroughly humiliated each other and come finally to rest. What more is there? The bar patrons had filled in around us again, buzzing with forgetful gin glee. But my other question still pestered.

Without turning to face him, I asked Hartman why he thought our CEO deleted my approvals from my page content.

Probably because it doesn't look good to be CEO and have someone around with a better screen, he said. Sipped. Gave not fucks.

He was right again.

I was despondent. More so than when I lost all of my accumulated positives, more so than when I was assumed to be trading blowjobs for angels, more so than when I pictured my mouth around a shriveled nipple drenched in Chanel. I clapped Hartman on the shoulder, thanked him and left the bar.

I knew I would be fired, so when I came in this morning, I brought donuts. It's okay, really. I'm sure I'll eventually find a job where I'm taken seriously.

holy property

Little Abbot walked past Old Hattie's every day and spit seeds into the bullet holes in the ground. Apple seeds, plum, peach, and cherry pits he plucked and tossed to click on the shells she'd shot. Old Hattie was always shooting up the yard to protect her formidable collection of plastic lawn ornaments from encroaching children. Abbot dreamed his discard would turn into trees. Root around the metal and cling like spider arms or hands of squid and push down until they could sprout up. He dreamed their tangled roots would crowd the metal sticks securing the pig, the lady and the gentlemen with their butts in the air, and the pink plastic flamingo with the graffitied penis on its face. The growth would push all of the atrocities out.

The discovery of the graffitied penis had been what prompted Old Hattie to begin employing the rifle. Even spitting pits was dangerous. She listened hard for disturbances to her plastic kingdom, shot a round at the slightest provocation or invasion of her property. The neighborhood boys couldn't confidently gauge her level of craziness so they had mostly stopped stealing her garden gnomes, pissing in her birdbath, and defacing her shiny pigs. She hadn't removed the penis-faced flamingo, though. She couldn't, it was her favorite.

Abbot had a route he walked carved out of convenience and certain looking and picking stops. He knew where mulberry trees and patches of sour clover grew. He liked the fruits his parents packed, but even better to eat out of the ground.

Hattie's was on his way home because of a detour past the movie theater. He liked to see what was playing, and even more he liked the fire trees. Bright red maples assaulted him in neat rows. Little round dirt clumps and shackles secured them to the parking lot islands. Their color drowned even the circus pizzazz of the theater's décor. Today at this very looking stop he'd spotted a huge bouquet of loosed balloons floating up. They were pastel and he thought the words "let go," and took in a gust of air, feeling fine.

He finished his fruit too early, but clutched the sticky pits in his hands for later use. He did not know why he felt so strongly that he had to fill each and every hole. But he did. This is why he knew the pink flamingo was Old Hattie's favorite. He'd spied her crying real tears onto its plastic feathers the day she found the penis face, and to boot a broken foot. He'd looked up from his hole hunting to stare at her. He'd stared for a moment too long and she caught him, one foot in her border. He'd moved toward her, thought to say something kind, but she glared at him and he froze.

She didn't trust people, Hattie. She'd hollered at everyone since time immemorial. But after that terrible day with the flamingo, she kept her gun trained. The police tried to take it away from her, but she had certain rights they couldn't deny. She was old but she wasn't batty, Hattie, at least not enough not to know her rights were undeniable. She hadn't harmed anyone. They left her to her obsessions.

She'd collected even more of the plastic horrors since the vandalism. Nary a blade of grass could be spied. There were squirrels with blood wounds, groundhogs, fluorescent butterflies, aliens, dinosaurs, dolphins, spinning opalescent headache makers, whirly gigs and talking coffee beans. The boy hated this so much.

He imagined giants tall as redwoods using the ornaments as toothpicks, laughing as gunshots tickled their toes. He imagined it all upturned, the yards and fences and houses, everything ugly pushed out by his enormous apple-born kings and queens. He saw lawnmowers hanging like earrings from stately oak faces, lacey leaf hair covering all of the poorly painted shutters that ever were. Abbot felt bad for Old Hattie in a way. But he wanted her penis-faced plastic flamingo with the broken foot to be a broach upon the cloud cap of the tallest pear tree that ever lived.

When he neared the monstrosity of the terrible lawn he spit on a pit to loosen its gummy stick, speeded his pace, then slowed to search out a solid hollow. He caught the beady eye of Hattie peering over the barrel from her window, startled, and instinctively aimed for it. He let go.

He didn't think himself the type to throw hard objects at old lady eyes, it was something his hand not his mind decided, at least that's what he decided. Hattie's happy trigger finger also made a decision. What happened could've been better than balloons, though it twisted his squirmy insides so hard he fell on his knees. The bullet met the thrown peach stone in mid air, exactly halfway between him and the old collector. It exploded too fast to see how its tiny bits filled hundreds of empty holes where nothing could grow.

A pinwheel twirled, Hattie spit, and Abbot's loss set him suddenly to standing. He took ten startled steps forward, and in his panic, grabbed the pink flamingo and placed it between his legs in a crude gesture. He pretended he was a furious giant. He pulled it up to his neck like a broach. He waved it up high like a flag. He was so frightened that he was shouting his biggest and angriest shouts, pumping his flamingo filled fist. Hattie cocked her gun again, looked the child in the eye, and shot her ornament right in its pink plastic heart. He let go.

Abbot dropped the stick that was no longer holding much atop it, shocked. That second bird-shattering shot, it burst something inside of him. Something he wasn't aware lived there. "But it was so pretty," he said, not understanding the words and feelings pouring from the popped casing of his hate.

Hattie came down from her perch to stand beside him. He crouched to stroke the splintered pink as his tiny tears fell in the dirt on dead seeds. The old woman met him on the ground, her skirt gathered and fanned around her like the leaf-laced hair of a giant and Abbot, vulnerable as he was, climbed onto her lap. His mouth frowned but he curled his body into a smile. She was reluctant. Still, she patted the boy's back amidst the wreckage of her most cherished possession. "So pretty," Abbot said again.

basic ten

Colin's job at the factory: Stick enormous metal comb into a deep rectangular tray of paste. Well, Colin called it paste. It was a papier-mâché type sludge, containing polymers to be sure and god knows what chemicals, but still smelling pleasantly like flour and water. Pleasantly at first. Anything pleasant becomes sickly if there's far too much of it.

Stick the comb in the center of the tray and pull to the right.

The unsifted paste has one purpose and the sifted paste another, Colin knows. What those purposes are, he cannot say. He took an interest at first in the hopes of gaining some satisfaction as to his contribution. All he discerned was that his factory sent products to other factories. The other factories would someday turn their products into something actual and useable. What Colin sifted with his metal comb was called Basic 10. Thank god the world had Colin, so that it could have its Basic 10.

He was a happy guy, Colin. He pumped his fists and regularly shifted from foot to foot. He grew his hair out a little long. He got friends out of houses and out to the bar, or sometimes off to an amusement park or a camping trip. His friends didn't necessarily respect him. For one thing, he was short. For another, he was always so damned happy. But they liked him. They responded to his yessing head and enthusiastic gesturing. Or perhaps it was his handsome face. Colin had a somewhat handsome face. Blue eyes, scruffy chin, laugh lines in becoming places. This was all fine and well. The combination of generally winning features that balanced Colin's niceness and shortness and won him favor with his friends and sometimes the ladies, on whom he performed an extraordinary amount of oral sex when he was dating one, did not go over as well in his workplace. For one thing: he didn't perform oral sex in the workplace. Good for Colin. For another, it was difficult to tell a joke when he'd been performing the same action for five or six hours. Even if he could retain his wits well enough, he couldn't really be heard. It was loud in there. Estephania, his nearest neighbor wore a bandana down over her ears and didn't speak much English anyway. He'd tried to connect in the beginning, using intro level Spanish he'd gleaned during a stint as a line cook. "Mas caliente, right?" She'd shaken her head and called him a pendejo under her breath. His other nearest neighbor was Bob. Bob sweat a lot. He was overweight because he'd thrown his back out doing construction. He was pissed that he now turned a switch on and off for a living because he'd once made homes. Bob might have talked to Colin but Colin got a sad feeling when he looked at Bob's half-mast eyes and drippy bald head. Luckily, Colin loved to watch the paste. Watching the paste was what kept him from leaving his job. Well, that and the fact that there weren't many jobs to be had out here in the sticks. Classic story: mom sick, dad absent, shuffle footed return to the old hometown. Tumbleweed.

Basic 10 secretly made Colin immensely happy. Not all the time. Colin smoked a bit of pot, but he wasn't nuts. It made him overflow with happiness only in certain moments. The strands of goo as they clung and pulled. The texture of sliding and ripping. Melted gray sheets falling over and into one another, the slime and spread, or treasures of small clumps of powder unmixed. There were layers that could be detected by the discerning eye. Wet layer over smooth layer. Colin sometimes wanted to put his whole arm into it. Feel the thick. Both arms. His face. Instead he pulled the big comb and watched shiny bubbles and swirling patterns in the left sludge and it made him sing.

If you liked it than you shoulda put a comb in it. Comb all ye faithful.

Another thing about Colin was his last name. Furth. Like the actor, but only almost. This annoyed him but not immensely. Many people share names and almost names. It's a fact of life.

Lastly, Colin had a crush. It was a strange crush and it happened in a strange way. He'd noticed that one of the list girls had an accident with her period. He was presented with a dilemma. Tell her, you embarrass her. Don't tell her, you expose her to more embarrassments and you expose others to similar dilemmas. Colin did the math and tapped her on the shoulder like a man. She turned her head around very slowly. She did everything very slowly. He watched her pupils adjust to him because he suddenly had the time. She was one of those people who had the power to slow you down. If you didn't slow down in her presence you would completely miss her. Plus, though he was usually a jittery guy, he wasn't in any rush to tell her there was blood on her pants. He watched her eyelids close slowly and open slowly and he watched her gently pull her clipboard to her chest. He felt protected by this other pace. He noticed her long eyelashes and pondered how dimples could exist on such a slender face.

Slender is an understatement. Gwen was a list girl, and all of the list girls were broomstick thin. Think Burkina Faso, subtract distended belly. Colin had always wondered if part of their job entailed reaching their hands and arms into a tiny corner to retrieve the floor manager's lost pens. He couldn't think of why the company only hired tall skinny women for these listing positions. They were fun to watch walk around, though, like floating thermometers. Dinosaur necks rising to peer above the floor like moons.

At this point, Colin did not know Gwen's name. He started there.

"Hi, I'm Colin—I don't think we've met formally," he squinted his eyes a smidge and extended his hand. She looked at it. Undid her fingers from her clipboard. Opened her hand. Reached out as if she were about to touch an infant, with utmost care. Placed her soft hand in his and allowed him to guide the duration of the greeting limply. Without thinking he brought his left hand up and gave her the old two-hander. He was as surprised as she was by the intimacy.

"Gwen," she said and her left eyebrow crept up. He let go.

"Furth. Like the actor," he said.

"Excuse me?" Gwen asked.

"Oh nothing, my last name. Listen," he was slow to start, "this is—"

"Mine is Hen."

"Gwen Hen?" He stifled a chuckle and smiled instead.

"Parents think they're cute," she said. "I don't tell people unless I have to." Her slow manner of speaking gave off the effect of her smoking a cigarette, the way a sultry movie character might, even though she wasn't. In a movie. Or smoking. Or seducing him intentionally. Probably not. He could feel himself wanting to spend his whole break with her. Once he told her what was up she would avoid him. He wondered if the problem was getting worse behind her. Pools of blood gathering and dripping. This had the odd effect of making him feel close to her rather than grossed out. He had never liked such a skinny woman before. He had never wanted to move so slow. Drip down walls and curl around teacups.

"Maybe they are cute," he said. "Their daughter is." WHOA. That sounded slimy. Colin wasn't slimy. But she was smiling! Starting to. Ever so lazily her lips wrapped themselves around her mouth. She chewed the bottom one. Her cheeks pinkened. She rubbed her long forefinger up and down her clipboard like it was the back of a napping cat ear. Colin's urge was to clap his hands together and make a joke or change the subject or hum a tune, but instead he stayed locked in. She made a sound. "Hm."

"Sorry," he said but kept staring.

"Why?" she asked.

"I have to go to the bathroom," he said. He said it because he was getting an erection and didn't want her to see. But then he remembered that she had to go to the bathroom too. And then she said—

"Me too."

SAVED by the power of suggestion! Yes. Except no, because the conversation was over. But yes, because it had gone well. Too well, maybe. Colin did not give oral sex in the workplace, but if you asked him he would not tell you what he did with the rest of his lunch break in a bathroom stall.

When he went back to his Basic 10 bins the ooze became torturously sexy to watch. His time in the bathroom had not broken the spell that had come over his body. He looked up in the hopes of seeing Gwen bob by. Repeat. Repeat. Finally a pair of brown spotted pants came into view. He was disappointed that she hadn't seen her problem when she went to the bathroom. Or maybe she just didn't have spare clothes in her locker. He was about to call to her but she turned around. It wasn't Gwen Hen. It was another list girl! The list girls are all bleeding, Colin thought. Cycles sync, he reasoned. He lowered his eyes to the churning muck. Pulled his comb.

Gwen Hen did come, ten to five. Colin had been mentally slow fucking the Basic 10 for hours and was in a sort of trance. It was Friday so people were already starting to pack up and trickle out. No one waited for the night shifters on Fridays. Estephania and Bob were shutting down and Colin only had two bins left. He was enthralled with a soft swirling when he felt her hand. He startled even though her hand was warm and placid. Looked up. Her pupils did their thing. Dazed blinking for both of them. Hi then hi. She kept her hand there. Before his brain could tell him not to, he slid his palm side up and held hers. She still kept her hand there. He rubbed the top of her hand with his thumb like a sloth might rub a hand. She still kept her hand there and moved her fingertips almost imperceptibly. To anyone but Colin.

"Is it hot?" she asked.

"Yes," he said without thinking.

"I want to put my hands in it," she said.

"Oh, you mean the B-10? No it's not hot."

She inched forward in time to a smile and laughed her sound. "Hm."

"Not at this station—at eighteen it would—

She brought his hand down. It was slippery. They touched each other's fingers in tender strokes, the glop running between thick and grey. Plasticine yogurt on skin. They avoided the blades, and went further down in the bin. Still eye contact until she closed her eyes. She made a low sound. They were elbow deep now with both hands.

That was how the first day of Colin's crush went. Which would seem not to qualify it as a crush with satisfaction granted and/ or imminent. But an odd thing happened after he and Gwen played in the B10. They washed their arms in the mess sink and once clean, walked away without exchanging telephone numbers or goodbyes. Colin had tried. Her attention laser beamed on the towel she was using to dry. Then her slow walk to the lot. He couldn't follow her like a puppy. He couldn't just break silence because silence was something to be entered into with an invitation in hand. So he watched her go with every fire his body knew how to make burning his brains out.

He sees her every day. Often she is bleeding and often she smiles. The smiles are a shared event, sometimes they seem to go on for hours. Sometimes they talk but Colin lets her initiate this. Not because he is shy. Colin isn't shy and maybe that's part of the problem. He feels cast out of the lot when near her, intensely aware of his clumsy noise and motion. He can only join her when she takes him down to that other universe where things are languid. He desires that universe so much that it makes him anxious and then he really can't pop the film over the entrance. So to speak. So he writes poetry. Drafts of emails he never sends to her company email address. Considers following her home but catches the inner stalker in him and gives him a firm talking to. Spends almost all of his lunch breaks in the bathroom or in his pickup truck, resorting to Power Bars for sustenance. When alone with the privacy of his body he can enter her pace. The rest of the time zip zip zips, arms of Colin flailing to grab onto something. Already a slender guy, he loses weight. He believes his hair to be falling out. Gwen Hen smiles and lists things. She bleeds like the others. Floats on her feet.

Well, what happens with crushes? The same thing happens every time, so there is almost no need to tell Colin's tale. Almost no need. He gets crushed of course, day in, day out. Other girls like him, fine young women who maybe wouldn't like him normally but he is emitting pheromones like a power washer. He doesn't notice them. He doesn't give oral sex to them, except for in one case involving copious amounts of alcohol. Ignores her calls afterward. Gwen Hen often seems oblivious to all of this, but he knows she's not. Her senses, so carefully groomed to take in one thing at a time, must feel the contours of each item they absorb in minute detail. He imagines how the grooves of every feeling are known to her. How she practically memorizes fingerprints. How she knows the underside of her tongue, the curves of the flop of flab between breast and armpit. Even if she's not conscious of it, she has to feel the attention coming at her like it's a runaway caboose. Plowing her down. She probably has just as much trouble entering Colin's universe, much as she would like to, much as she's lonely. So they touch fingertips across the divide. They wave handkerchiefs of hello and farewell from their platforms, his is red and flapping furiously, hers is blue and just drifts.

Unfortunately the list girls start disappearing. This is a real problem for both of them, Colin Furth and Gwen Hen alike. No one knows where they are going, but there are fears. When you work in a factory there are fears. There is also a fierce denial that disguises itself as loyalty, that disguises itself as not thinking about it. Real friendships are rarely formed and information is hard to come by in a noisy place where everyone is involved in repetitive motions. Dulled minds still notice the difference between ten tall bobbing heads and five. Dulled minds don't know what to do with that observation, however. Estephania is bleeding too. Her forehead is creased.

A meeting is called. Everyone assembles and Rick, who Colin calls Rick Roll, announces that the company is experiencing cutbacks. It's as if buttons are undone after a meal. Everyone feels better because this is a lesser worry than the one previously denting the skin of their faces. There had always been a lot of turnover. Colin had managed to find a place to sit right next to Gwen Hen. At the news, she placed her hand on his. It was as if the zipper came down too. Full belly out. Full breath.

After everyone got up they remained sitting like that. There was buzzing in Colin's body like a fluorescent light. Gwen Hen's too. He had the odd desire to lick her finger, and the odd idea that she wouldn't mind. He didn't, though. He put his head on her shoulder. They breathed.

Gwen Hen did not come in the next day, or the day after that. Colin paced a lot. Colin drank a lot of whiskey. Colin finally sent some of his emails. Gwen Hen did not respond. Rick Roll was not at liberty to disclose information. Estephania had given Hernandez a package. Estephania had swatted Colin on the arm. Estephania stopped showing up. Bob seemed fine. Bob went on with it. On. Off. On. Off.

The company was moving its factories to Mexico. Memos were disbursed, meetings ceased. People nodded. People understood. Colin put his arms in the Basic 10, still hoping against doom. What could you do? People understood.

our acts together

At eighty-two years old, my grandmother decided to go to law school. We all congratulated her. I made trophy-winning hands at her. She beamed.

There can be nothing wrong with a grandmother going to law school. It will keep her mind active, we thought. It will be like a constant crossword puzzle! What a wonderful decision, what a badass grandmother, an exemplar for other grandmothers.

Upon further consideration, though, we realized that she would probably never practice law. Law school takes quite awhile, even for a limber mind. She would go into substantial debt that she would never have time to pay off. She'd already taken out a second mortgage on her house, she'd retired years ago, her pension wasn't much to speak of, her husband was long dead. These were difficult subjects to breach with her, though, so no one did.

Furthermore, she'd already begun to memorize legal codes by the time we realized against our hope how ill advised a plan this was that she'd hatched. I have to study the acts now, she kept repeating, I have to prepare. I'd been helping her make piles of multicolored paper labeled and cross-labeled. She was becoming facile with acts in acronyms. The CALM Act, the CLASS Act, the PATRIOT Act—*Commercial Advertisement Loudness Mitigation Community Living Assistance Services and Supports Providing Appropriate Tools Required to Intercept and Obstruct Terrorism!*—she rattled, breathless, placing blue stickers in the corners of these slips, which meant **success**. Then she'd make a decision. Pile the paper squares in their home colors by **subject**? Pile them all mixed-colored into **success** or **needs review**? Alphabetize?

These kids are going to know these things. I have to know them too.—They are? Are you sure?—I have to have a grasp.— Okay, but everyone's all worried, Dad said—You can tell my son to shove it. Have a little respect for your mother, tell him, Jesus.

I could only assume she was devising a consistent system within what looked like shards of rainbows. I ran around in the paper piles trading color for color, doing just what she said. Her legs didn't work so well anymore. No, put it on top of PACT—What's PACT?—Prevent All Cigarette Trafficking— I blew out smoke—Ha—No what color?—Indigo! Come on you're a young man!—Okay!—I don't want to die without seeing my country—Wait what, Grandma?—You heard me.

I asked her if she wanted to go on a road trip. No, she didn't want to go on a road trip. She waved her hand around the room strewn with sheets of crimson, gold, sea green, pewter. She said *this* and flicked her wrist at the mounds. This is my country. Then she stood up and paced, which she doesn't do very often, legs and all. The floor isn't working she said. We need a wall. We'll need several walls, I told her. I didn't want my grandmother to die, period, certainly not without seeing what she needed.

Basement? Garage? Attic? Not big enough, as it turns out, to house the sight of a grandmother's country. Grandmothers care about their countries. I looked into warehouse space while Grandma collected rejection letters from the top tier schools she'd applied to. She was a sport about it. She adjusted her horizons and reapplied. She included photos of our code collage beginnings in her second round of applications. I told her it was a bad idea. They're gonna think you're nuts, and you already have your age working against you—Oh shush, I'm diligent.

We settled on a storage unit because we remembered that my dad had one. He really only used it for files, his half hearted model ship collection, and his old easy boy. We suckered him into the loan after he'd had a few Dewars. The next day we put the stacks in plastic bins and hauled them in a mid-sized moving van. A stencil graffiti-making friend taught me the values of wheat paste, a roller, and a ladder. We left the garage style door open for sunlight, and stuck our acts up on the wall.

Sometimes maintenance men and other key holders peeked in and we took to handing out copies of acts that suited their personalities. I'd roll them up like diplomas and watch their confusion as they read about "Seeing Eye Dogs on Railroads" (guy with thick glasses) or "Juvenile Justice and Delinquency Prevention" (shady looking kid with his mom) or "Sunshine

Act" (Birkenstock wearer) while Grandma and I applauded. They'd always leave us alone after that. Well, with the exception of the janitor, Martin, who gave us organizational tips in exchange for cigarettes and enticed us into the occasional card game on our breaks. He liked his diploma. It was the Strategic and Critical Materials Stock Piling Revision Act. It suited him. Boy could that man play cards. Guess what we played for? Yep. He "stock piled" almost all of the Department of Commerce and Department of Military. If you're not familiar, that's a real lion's share there. It was all in good fun, though. He'd give them back at the end of the game while he pretended to get back to work. Janitors in Storage Facilities don't have much of a grind, really. But me and Grandma did. More than we knew.

I began to realize that I shouldn't have trusted the consistency of Grandma's system. The addition of walls to our work clarified the lack of clarity we'd been engaging in. At first we organized all of the acts in vertical strips with horizontal color connections. Consider the construction of this little rainbow, AKA **Truth Strip**!:

Truth in Fur Labeling Act of 2010
Pub. L. 111–313, Dec. 18, 2010, 124 Stat. 3326
Short title, see 15 U.S.C. 69 note **(dark red)**

Is this someone's job? Fur labels?—Hand me the tape?

Truth in Lending Act
Pub. L. 90-321, title I, May 29, 1968, 82 Stat. 146 (15 U.S.C. 1601 et seq.)
Short title, see 15 U.S.C. 1601 note **(burnt orange)**

Ha—Haha—Hahaha.

Truth in Lending Act Amendments of 1995
Pub. L. 104–29, Sept. 30, 1995, 109 Stat. 271
Short title, see 15 U.S.C. 1601 note **(burnt orange)**

Haha.

Truth in Lending Class Action Relief Act of 1995
Pub. L. 104-12, May 18, 1995, 109 Stat. 161
Short title, see 15 U.S.C. 1601 note **(burnt orange)**

Ha.

Truth in Lending Simplification and Reform Act
Pub. L. 96-221, title VI, Mar. 31, 1980, 94 Stat. 168
Short title, see 15 U.S.C. 1601 note **(burnt orange)**

Hm.

Truth in Mileage Act of 1986
Pub. L. 99-579, Oct. 28, 1986, 100 Stat. 3309 **(undecided)**

This old bag has gotten a lot of mileage, that's the truth.—Ew,
Grandma.

Truth in Regulating Act of 2000
Pub. L. 106-312, Oct. 17, 2000, 114 Stat. 1248 (5 U.S.C. 801 note)
(undecided)

No way, no way are you operating the roller anymore, Grandma. Look how clumpy!—But I like the sound it makes.

Truth in Savings Act
Pub. L. 102–242, title II, subtitle F (Sec. 261 et seq.), Dec. 19, 1991,
105 Stat. 2334 (12 U.S.C. 4301 et seq.)
Short title, see 12 U.S.C. 4301 note **(sky blue)**

I need a nap.

Truth in Securities Act
See Securities Act of 1933 **(light purple)**

Me too.

I had begun to employ the use of paint to dab blobs of referenced note colors next to the scrawls of acts lined up and glued in stripes. It was to connect them with acts they were related to, but some of them were across the room. Nonetheless we both admired how the storage room had begun to look like a vertical sunset horizon, dotted with multicolored stars. We laughed a lot during the early weeks. All the while, though, I thought my grandmother was making sense of things. I certainly wasn't. But she had seemed so sure (and then she didn't) when she said things like: No, put the LIFE Act (Legal Immigration Family Equity!) and its Amendments next to the Fair Sentencing Act of 2010. It seemed logical enough. But then all the "Fair" acts, Access to Foster Care, Accurate Credit Transactions, Equitable Tobacco Reform, Credit and Charge Disclosure, Credit Billing, Credit Reporting, Debt Collection Practices, Housing, Housing Amendments, Labor Standards, Labor Standards Amendments (1949, 1955, 1961, 1966, 1974, 1977, 1985, 1989), Minimum Wage, Packaging and labeling, Sentencing, Share Refugee, Trade, Trade in Auto Parts, Treatment for Experienced Pilots, Music Licensing, & Contact Lens Consumers were interrupted by LIFE, an acronym. It was an aesthetic disharmony, and as chief paste person and paint dabber I had begun to invest in the look of the thing above all. While the disharmony was one that was admittedly interesting, it prompted me to ask Grandma: why?

What if instead of strips we make pictures?—Okay. Like mnemonic devices?—Whatever. I just need to see it. All together.

She stared off at the far right wall and we simultaneously began placing all of the Marine Mammal Protection Acts in a pond shape in vivid clear-day blue.

It was fun at first. We felt we were really on to something.

We had a section shaped like a cash register, one shaped like a baby, a house, a car, and a hammer. But again, inconsistencies emerged, this time while we were building a justice scale out of the act titles.

Grandma? Grandma, why are we putting the LIFE act with the Fair Acts and not in the house, or with PACE and TREAD and all of the other acronyms?

The acronyms were shaped like an old balding head in a far corner.

Protecting America's Competitive Edge Through Energy Transportation Recall Enhancement, Accountability, and Documentation, she recited in a tired tone, when an actual bald man waltzed into the storage room, my dad. Funny enough, he stood right under the acronyms of his likeness. I gave him a nod. He folded his arms in front of him.

What are you doing in here?—Oh shut up, Bob, I'm trying to see my country.—The storage company called and told me to check my belongings.—Why?—They said squatters had gotten in.—Ha.—Martin?—Probably.—He thinks he's funny.—Who's Martin?—Janitor.—A real card shark.—He likes pranks.—This place is a mess.

We looked up. The largest wall was chipped and bearing its particleboard. A square of light illuminated our crooked paper gun that suddenly looked more like a penis. He was right. It was a total mess.

Where's my easy chair?—Oh get out will you? We won't hurt your precious La-Z-Boy.

My father shifted around for a few more minutes, taking stock of his ships in the corner. He was no match for his mother, though. He complimented her diligence on the way out.

See?—Ha.

I thought her son's compliment had pleased her. But once he'd gone I caught her staring up at the rocking chair of Older Americans Acts while I searched for a roll of paper towels. I was about to say something when Martin strutted in. Grandma marched right up to him and clapped a PATRIOT Act diploma into his hands with a customary side smirk. I applauded. Martin tied a little ribbon around his broom and handed it to Grandma. I applauded.

"So much diplomacy," I said.

"Very punny," Grandma said in a tone that implied how unfunny this was to her.

Martin was pleased with himself. He tried to lure us into a game of spades but Grandma broomed him from the room shouting *Ever heard of Privacy?*

She went back to the Older Americans with her chin resting on her fist. I chose a spot to wipe nearby. When I saw her fingers press into her forehead and her face crumple into her hand, I interrupted her.

Grandma?

"It's all so confusing," she said.

She lifted her head and stared directly into my eyes in a rare gesture. Her eyes welled up. I couldn't take that. I told her not to lose heart, that she was doing great, and I put my arm around her.

"What if I never see it?" she asked. "What if I die and I never see it?"

"What do you mean? You haven't even started school yet," I said. I lightly side punched her arm. She looked up at me again and rolled her eyes. I guess another round of rejections had come. I couldn't believe the words that came out of my mouth then but I said, "Let's just start over again," and we did. This was school.

The next layer of acts we organized by time. It was ugly, but at least it told a story.

the best deal

The girl watched the boy. The boy had in one hand a box and in the other hand a bird. The boy had no reason to give her anything at all, but here he was. The girl had mainly been minding her own business. She'd just been sitting in the frosty atrium, looking out of the windows at the snow or down at the grey floor, up at the trees sprinkled inside. There were no windows really. The whole room was made of glass. It was calming after the clamor of the show. She was admiring the bird, a big green thing, species of some island. She'd only seen a bird like that in pictures. The boy must have caught her staring because he walked right over.

"I'll give it to you," he said. Just like that. She snapped her fingers and slapped her fist.

"Really?" She worked to conceal the joy threatening to spread across her face.

"Actually, I'll give you a choice. You can have the bird, or what I have here in this box."

He was handsome despite his ratty traveling clothes and five o' clock shadow. Only a few years older than she, it looked like, seventeen maybe. He wore a cap and smiled like a salesman, but his eyes pointed down.

The bird, she thought instantly, of course, the bird. But she didn't say. She wanted to see what was in the box. She wasn't sure if she should trust him to really give her anything. Maybe he was a trickster.

"Why are you going to give me something?" she asked.

"Lighten my load."

"Hm."

They paused.

"Well, can I see what's in the box?"

He nodded and took a cloth from his pocket, a white rag with two blue stripes. The box was an oblong rectangle about the size of a large shoebox, with the kind of lid that slides open—no hinges—no clasps. He slid the lid through the slats, and to the girl's dismay it contained what appeared to be dead animals. He began taking them out, one by one, and wiping them with the cloth. She was about to say, "the green bird, please," when the dead bird he'd taken out of the box and cleaned, a parrot, gave its feathers a shake and struggled to its feet. It waddled toward a tree. The boy was already busy wiping the next bird, a cockatiel. The girl's mouth was open. She shut it. A bead of sweat dripped down her ribs. The cockatiel shook itself off and inspected the marble floor and then a soil square holding a hickory sapling. Poor thing kept falling on its side like it was drunk.

"This one is extinct," he explained. He held a furry thing with a monkey tail.

"It smells like formaldehyde," she said, trying to keep up. She was afraid to ask questions and break the spell of his generous mood.

"There's some formaldehyde in the fluid, to preserve them while they are dead."

"Dead?"

"Well they don't exactly die. They freeze, kind of."

Okay, she was ready to ask questions now, but the monkey was waking up. It lifted its head and stared straight at her with huge and glassy baby-seal eyes. It climbed onto her lap. She stroked its thick fur. It had large hind legs, curved at the thigh like a dog or a bunny, a white stripe down the middle of its back from its head to the tip of its tail, and big ears sticking out. She hugged him, he breathed warm air on her neck, and she set him on the ground. He lumbered over to the tree the parrot was now perched in and started climbing with slow swoops and labored breath.

"I'll take the box," she said, and felt shrewd. She'd gotten the best deal. She couldn't help but say it, "These must be worth a fortune." Though even as the words slipped out she knew she could never sell them. Her gut twisted with regret that she'd even imagined it, watching them now with their awkward attempts at being animals. She looked up and watched the healthy green bird flying big free circles through the dome.

The boy explained the logistics of "freezing" and "unfreezing" the animals. It was simple. You doused them in this fluid and shut the lid. Once you shut the lid they became very much like dead—then when you wanted to revive them, you wiped them off and brought them out in the fresh air. "This way you can bring them everywhere. No nuisance." She barely paid attention. She didn't want to make her animals go dead in the box ever again.

The boy called the green bird down from the atrium sky, and it rested on his shoulder. They went on their way.

She stared at her monkey who was falling from branch to branch, clumsy with torpor, and it filled her with love. The birds just sat still, one on the ground, one in the tree. They stared ahead at nothing. She walked over and petted them.

It must have been a good ten minutes before she realized that the show was likely over. Her family was probably looking for her in the lobby. The reality then struck her with force—she had no choice but to put the animals back in the box. Her parents would never let her keep two birds and an extinct monkey in their polished house. They wouldn't even let her have goldfish. They would make her sell them. Someone would pay a lot of money to cut them open and see how they worked. This person would act friendly, but wouldn't be.

The animals were easy to capture. They didn't put up any fight at all. She took her time stroking and tickling them. She whispered that it would be okay. Her heart tore in her chest when she doused the cloth, hoping to get it right. She watched them go limp under the effect of the fluid, then stiffen. They didn't seem to be breathing as she arranged them in the box, kissing each one. She tried to make them comfortable. She blew on their fur, drying the mix of tears and fluid. Maybe she would keep them in the box forever, just to avoid this feeling in her. She told herself she was saving their lives. But a part of her went with them into the box, hard and dead. She closed the lid. She stuffed the box into her backpack, wrapping it with her extra sweater.

On her way out she noticed another little girl on the far side of the room. She wondered how long she'd been watching. She remembered the boy's words about lightening his load. He *was* a trickster. She crossed the atrium toward the little girl, wondering if yet another little girl was watching, and thought she'd try being truthful when she struck her deal. But the little girl ran away terrified, and every time the box moved in her bag, every step she took, was a reminder.

When she was safely home with her family, she hid the box under her bed. She hoped to forget, but never could. Sometimes at night when everyone was sleeping she took the animals out to cuddle. But when it was time to put them back she stiffened each time, and more and more went dead in the box. Eventually, it was simpler just to leave them be.

even the line

There were two picnic tables end to end under the tent. At each place setting was a rectangular block of wood slightly more petite than a place mat, the thickness of a porterhouse steak. In each upper right hand corner of each wooden place setting there was a cup-sized hollow, and in each cup-sized hollow, a smooth stone mug was jammed. Each stone mug contained a silver stirring spoon. The handles of the spoons were twisted like metal twizzlers, or if they spun or had color, the red and white indicators of barbershops. But here were no barbershops, here was an un-begun feast.

If it were night, headlights would illuminate everything from behind so that silhouettes would become so specific that you could make out the thin spiked wisps of your conversation partner's ear fuzz. Except there were no headlights, because it was day, and you didn't have a conversation partner. You sat there all alone, puzzling at how to sip from stuck mugs. Soon people would arrive. Would you really expect them to lift an entire block of wood to bring a cup to their lips? Field gnats made drunken daredevil dives around your face.

You went inside the house where the only blocks of wood rested on the tops of legs or shelves and there were no gnats save one or two. The soothing presence of your wife baking her prized peanut muffins relaxed you. Her hair was warm and sunlit around her face. She smiled at the sight of you and handed you a spoon to lick. You could stare at Emma all day and be calm. But she wasn't much of a conversation partner these days. She said what was expected to be said, like you did lately. She did what was expected to be done, like you did lately. Still, her smile. What kind of man would give that up?

She was making whisking noises and whipping motions. Measuring cups and broken eggs threatened to make a choppy chalk coated music, click-click, soft goes the cook. But they didn't make music, not the eggshells. They just sat there. You decided to just sit there too, like an eggshell. You weren't in the mood for company anymore, but it was no use. Company was coming. How often does a man celebrate the end of a ten-year apprenticeship?

How often does a man become a master? Still that phrase made you laugh. As if you had yourself a herd of sawdust elves careening beneath your jig saw. You didn't. It was private most of the time, woodwork. You wouldn't even be a master yet if old Mr. Peterburden hadn't had a heart attack, keeled over onto the scroll saw, and died. You would have been his obedient six-foot sawdust elf-giant for ten or eleven years more. But as it was he did keel over.

The funeral had been a disaster. Old Mr. Peterburden had broken a few pacemakers over the years as it turned out. You'd suspected he had mistresses; shy knocks would come, knuckles sliding between taps on the chipping door to the shop. You'd worried after splinters on the knuckles of pining, wrinkled lady-hands on multiple occasions. Would have thought it was just one woman he was sleeping with, and who could blame the old buzzard, the wife had been gone for years, except you'd spied so many versions of whispered consolations on the way to your truck. This recipient had blue hair, that one had a penchant for neon colored t-shirts, this one used a cane (and swatted you on the toosh with it once), that one was in possession of a pair of hearty breasts much smoother than the spotty frowning face they matched. Old Peterburden had had himself a second wind. Who could blame him?

Unfortunately his mistresses all showed up to his funeral, and they did blame him—vocally—into microphones. The sobbing heard in the halls was because he'd lived as long as he had, not because he'd died. You had attempted to bring a spirit of honor to the occasion by installing some of Peterburden's best cabinets around the funeral parlor. One woman had opened the latch of a flex cut beauty, European Oak, and screamed her head off into it. "Rage therapy," she said when she was done, "It's the primal scream." Her face was red and sweat dewed the sides of her tangelo lips. A few of the others nodded their heads in solidarity and patted her shoulders. "We learned it at the Y."

"What are you thinking about, Sweetie?" Emma asked.

"Remember the funeral?" you asked her.

"Oh, that." She smiled. "What a trip."

"Yeah," you sighed.

"Oh, Honey. Are you feeling sad?" she asked.

"Yes." You were suddenly. She kissed the top of your forehead and raked your hair with her fingertips. "I think I'll go lie down for a nap," you said.

"Oh, but Babe, the guests will arrive soon."

It wasn't your idea to have a party in the first place. You didn't even have friends really, except for Jimmy Downs the lumber salesman, and Nick Notary your childhood friend who had slowly retreated from society to make electronic music on Garage Band and care for his five ailing dogs. He said he was coming but you doubted it.

The party was an idea concocted by the funeral mass over post wake cocktails. "There must be a celebration," someone had said, "For you," because everyone assumed you would inherit the woodshop; everyone assumed you were the new master in town. The idea caught and ice cubes clinked assent. Now relative strangers were coming to your house to sip from woodblocks. It was disquieting.

"We want to see your work," Lucille, the one with the fluorescent color obsession had said, "You'll have to show us your stuff!" Even with her bright orange lipstick dotted with cornbread crumbles, she'd managed to rally some local excitement for the unveiling of your pieces. The old ladies had all nodded, pledged their desperation to purchase new woodwork. You had, in fact, been working on a project. Your stomach fluttered.

"Go get it ready," Emma said, "Go on."

"What if no one comes?" you asked her.

"They'll come," she said, and bopped you on the nose with her spoon.

"What if someone gets lost or freaks out?" you asked.

"Don't be silly."

You did feel silly though. You gave Emma a scared dog look and a whimper on the way to the door. Doors. Doors and doors. That's all. You walked out into the backyard, turning for a second to view your squat little pink house, wondering if you could still back out.

There had been the question of rooms, what the doors would lead to. You'd dreamed of creating all sorts of environments one could wander into. You'd dreamed that the environments would be so richly patterned that some people wouldn't even go on. But as it was, it was perhaps more truthful. Just doors. Simple ones, ugly ones, hollow ones, heavy ones, elaborate ones. You edged your way into the field.

Blast the wind. You shook your fist self-mockingly. One of the sheets had come down already. You beheld your grand plan and it seemed much more pathetic than it had at three o'clock in the morning, stringing and stringing the sheet hallways. Hundreds of freestanding doors (one hundred and forty three, to be exact) resting on flats, opening into each other, connected by tunnels made from white sheets, the scope at least, was impressive.

There were details you liked. Sometimes, if one walked through a tunnel in this labyrinth, they would have only one door to choose from. Sometimes, the tunnel would have three to five doors and they would all be different. One might be painted in a bright color; one might be gothic, one art nouveau, one simple pine with a golden knob. One might have a poster of Bob Marley tacked to it. (You thought this was a humorous touch.) Choices would have to be made, the doors would be contemplated. Did one want to get to the center or try to find a way out? Mahogany or maple? Smooth or ornate? Forward, back, left, right, in, out. To the center? If so, why?

This wasn't the best test audience since your guests were almost all geriatric. The perimeter doors begged to be locked once the walk began—to limit options—but you had no interest in giving anyone a heart attack. You'd considered giving out exacto knives as party favors. This way your guests could cut the sheets if they became lost or claustrophobic. But then you'd had visions of accidents, walker trauma bloodbaths. Really, seeing Peterburden's face cut up like that had been enough for a lifetime. You'd been the one to find him. You had put your hand on his scalp, what was left of his hair. You would leave the doors unlocked.

You fastened the fallen sheet. You tested the endurance of the lighter flats, adjusted sandbags. You sniffed the bouquet of lilies Emma had placed in a vase on the table by the entrance. They were leftover from the funeral, but amazingly still fresh. All was well. It would be fun you told yourself.

You heard a car horn being tapped on from down the street. Someone was announcing their arrival. You supposed you could still bail. You could pass the wooden place settings off as your life's work. You were passing the labyrinth of doors off as yours, after all, when really, it might have been Peterburden's idea. You shifted your weight from foot to foot. Did it matter? It might have been your idea. You had these memories but you couldn't distinguish their finer points, the timing. The moments fogged and conflated.

You went over it again as you walked toward the chipping house. You'd had that vision, the first epiphany you'd ever been able to articulate, if vaguely. It happened back when you lost your aunt, uncle, and father in only three years. You were only twenty. You didn't have the resources to deal with a death wave, the distance. None of them had accomplished anything they'd set out to accomplish before they died. The news had come about Dad. When the phone was placed on the handle, your little brother had fallen into your arms too weak to stand, the hardest part. After several hours the collective grief tide had rolled in for a moment, and you'd taken the quiet and gone outside. The first thing you noticed was a dead squirrel. It alarmed you that there could be a dead squirrel topping things off, at this particular moment, right beside the step. You stared at its corpse for a few minutes, perfectly intact. There was nothing missing from this squirrel but the movement, the air going in and out. You left the absent little body and decided to rest on a patch of grass underneath a bush and a few small trees. It was raining but you didn't care. The music of the drops falling from leaf to leaf and into your eyebrows lulled you into a trance. The dripping was a symphony of subtlety, sound more complex than you ever could have guessed with so much of it so soft. You were appalled at how intricately profound small moments could be, while life as a whole, life individually, retained its unblinking, meandering pattern of meaninglessness. So constant. You saw life, the big-L life, visually as a maze, and you saw yourself wandering it, so small, no reason to keep going except to feel like maybe you'd beaten the game of it for a minute, or the curiosity of trying another door, rooms containing illusions of progress like fruit baskets with notes attached, written in fine penmanship and addressed to you, but finally nothing, at the center nothing, not even the *choice* that had so consistently defined it thus far, no more doors, game over. There was no way to stop playing for any real period of time. There were brief moments when you were snatched up above the hedge somehow into a fleeting aerial view. But they were over so fast. You resigned yourself to waiting to be snatched, to learn how to snatch yourself. To your adult mind it seemed somewhat simple, but at the time this maze metaphor was a real revelation.

You lit up a raisin tasting cigarette when you got to the back door of your house, because you'd taken them up again, and because you needed to buy some time to remember. You sat on your steps.

When you went back to work after the death parades you'd confessed the results of your existential crisis to Peterburden. He was your conversation partner.

He would sip his black coffee and put his frail folded face into his furry hands, he would invade your soul with his droopy little red rimmed eyes that could stare right into your solar plexus.

He once told you about a rural community that worshipped a chair that had fallen out of a zeppelin and landed in front of a church. He mentioned things like that.

"It's just a maze," you told him when you returned to work, and you told him why. You told him that maybe love could give you an aerial view, but not much else, you weren't sure what else. You blushed. Then you blushed more because of the blush. You said love was pretty rare. He shook his head. He didn't say much. He was an intelligent man; he knew when to be quiet. Quiet was conversation too.

About a year or two later (here's where it gets fuzzy, time is such a bear), during his switch from primarily doors to primarily cabinets, he came in, placed his beat-up leather bag on the table, and said that it was time to complete his life's ambition: A labyrinth of doors. He said he would need your help. Did he say that he would need your help? He did.

Whose idea was it? And does it matter?

He never completed it. He had lots of sex and then keeled over onto the scroll saw. Maybe he had an intuition that his time was almost up—the way animals do. Because in the intervening five years he explained to you the workings of his dream. He showed you unfinished plans, coffee stained drafts. The opened doors would create the turns and tunnels. Closed doors could be opened to change the curvature of the hallways. There would be nothing at the center.

It was more complicated than you would think, crafting shifting tunnels out of only frames and doors. You had to rig up sheets instead. You'd need thousands of doors to do it right, millions to even come close to doing it to any respectable scale. But at least you'd done something.

You leaned your head against the worn little house. You wanted to do him honor. You loved him, even if he wrapped your epiphany into the steel wool of his own ambition. He wired up a final legacy from whatever raw materials were around, like you. How could you blame him? Now you were stuck with it, with him, with you. Dead people.

You opened the door and went inside. It was Sherri Brady who had arrived and she was already yucking it up in the kitchen with a cup of tea in her hand when you came in. Emma was good like that.

"Oh if it isn't the man of the *hour*! Come, come, hugs, hugs!" Sherri was a little younger than the mistresses Peter-burden, maybe sixty-five. She'd done his taxes, and as far as anyone knew, she'd not been scorned. She was squat and wore a purple suit. On her blazer she'd pinned a golden cornucopia.

"Sherri, thanks for coming," you paused and stared at her broach. "Emma treating you alright?"

"Oh she's a *dear*, a real *dear*. Lucky man! You are a lucky man, Mr. Straich."

"Indeed," you said, locking eyes with your wife. "But please, Otto."

"Oh, I just love that name. The two of them! Otto and Emma, Otto and Emma, I could say that all day long, I really could."

You smiled. You heard another car pulling onto the grass outside.

"Another guest!" Sherri said and stood with you.

The three of you walked awkwardly to the door together, glad to take the pressure of small talk off. At the doorway you all stopped, silently negotiating who would turn the blue glass knob. You did, you swung it open.

Five women were laboring themselves out of a Dodge. The mistresses of Thousand Oaks Court and Sycamore Landing, the twin retirement communities up Chatham, had arrived. Vernie, Bet, Waverly, Jean, and Lucille, wiggled, scooted, and grunted their way out of the vehicle, knocking purses, holding hands, squealing and crossing themselves. Lucille screamed, "Don't mind us, Ott Blott!" the other women laughed hysterically at this, "Ott Blott," they echoed, squeezing their legs together and holding their guts. "We take awhile but it's worth the wait!" They found hilarity in that statement as well.

You went down to help, Sherri and Emma followed. "Why don't we bring them straight to the tent," you said.

"A *tent!*" Lucille hollered.

"How wonderful!" Jean, the slight, agreeable one said.

"For the clowns," Big Bet said dryly, sending the ladies into stitches again.

"Clowns!" they gasped and repeated as they finally wedged out of the Dodge and started toward the tent.

The sun was coming down. A pleasant glow made the two tables less medieval looking despite the woodblock settings. You were glad for this.

"Oh how *interesting*," Sherrie said.

"Did you make these?" and, "Are these for sale?" and "Gosh I would love to have one of these for my apartment," and "It wasn't the old geezer, was it? Because I'm not eating off of anything his slimy hands touched!" Murmurs of assent.

"Oh, but my mug is stuck!"

"Is yours?"

"Ladies, this must seem terribly rude," you interrupted, "but I need to excuse myself for a few minutes." Terribly? Sometimes you started talking like your company. Everyone lifted brows to look.

Emma raised her eyebrows highest at you. "I have to fix something," you told her. She picked up from there. She was reliable like that.

"He's such a perfectionist," she told the crowd. "He probably wants to put some finishing touches on his display. We'll just get started without him." You were already walking away at a clip.

You'd broken into a sweat. You stopped by the garage to get two exacto knives. You could probably be seen from the tent but you didn't care. Your feet sucked into a muddy patch but you suctioned them back and blundered on.

Your entry into doors: wood. Doors were large enough and simple enough not to upstage the intricacy of the grain, you could trace the fibers with your fingers. Wood was a wonder, how as a child you saw so many faces in it, lopsided dogs, raging mothers, introspective godheads wearing glasses, melting queens with outstretched arms. You wondered if all of the world's fairytales had come from dreamers losing themselves in the knots and burls of their bedroom doors, creation myths born, perhaps, from staring into stumps. The mind blowing beauty of the colonization of fungi looping enigmatic web work, spalting the splinters, reminders of ecosystems born of ecosystems, the fragile exchange, the play of it all, right there, circling your hand as you turn the handle.

You had to meet the wood when you worked it, respond to its warps and twists, take aesthetic instruction from its touch, soft or hard. The heart shakes, friend or foe? Would they split or would they hold, feathering into anemones, a record preserved in stain, all of the fossils of all the world, spied in preview in a fine chatoyence? Decisions.

Decisions easily made because you hadn't had to lead. The wood led. Peterburden led.

You took a last look before you started, stared at the rigging that had taken you all week, working into the wee hours of the morning. It was ridiculous what you were about to do, you knew, but you would do it anyway.

You started slicing the fabric tunnels of the labyrinth with both hands. You couldn't help but think of the old man as you cut. You went at it hard and fast like a fat angry tomcat, razor blades for claws. You thought of him still, like you do of the dead, like they are right next to you, whether you believe that or not, sliding blade along seam, ripping with your hands for the feel of the pull and zip once a slice started, nails aching against resistance, you saw his face in the mess of stringing white, tore at the fabric like a lip, snapped strings like metatarsals, making it over. Sweat felt good amongst cotton sheets, and tears too. They wiped you dry while you worked down to the thread, burning off the patches that clung to staples. You wanted every last bit of connective tissue. You wanted nothing left.

When the maze had finally been fully dismembered you lugged all the sheet piles clumped by the doors and dumped them into one tall pile. You'd have to hide them.

Peterburden had once taken a compliment from a buyer that was yours, weak for praise. You had made that damn pie rest, not him. At least he shared the profit when it was purchased but that wasn't the point, was it? Tiny traces of cloth still hung from some of the frames, and you did your best with the Zippo again, picturing the shop, which you hadn't been back to yet, with its acorn smell, its filthy windows that let the light in, spotted and perfect. You took the doors you'd fashioned out of their strange circle and placed them in a straight line across the yard, door by door: your life's work.

You imagined him in some heaven of dusty tables, shaking his head, smirking from the eyes. You enjoyed the feeling of pushing your diaphragm down hard in order to lift the heavy doors up. You could maybe expel him this way, pushing down hard. You thumbed the edge of the ripple maple, remembered the day he taught you how to use the rasp and the riffler, how he corrected your shoots, hovering with patience while you learned to split, chuckling at your lines. You were remembering his mastery, true mastery. Even the way he touched his tools with his fingertips before he used them had taught you, the way he grunted when you said something dumb. You evened the line. He broke hearts, Peterburden, including yours. But true teachers mess up, you guessed, you missed him. You guessed you weren't ready. You rested for a minute.

The line of doors was long, much, much longer than you would've imagined. They spanned the entire field. By the time you were done it was full-blown night. It had been hours, you had missed your party, but you could only shrug. You wouldn't have been able to eat anyhow. Grief had become more tedious with age. It was something to tend to after the dishes, a chore to cross off of the to-do list. An impending responsibility, "Well, I guess I better pencil in some grief then." But how it pressed if you forgot to get to it. You welcomed the loss of appetite this time. You needed it, because death should keep its rightful place as special, bigger than work. You pulled the truck up a little, parked it and turned the headlights on so there was some light. Maybe you could sell these damn doors. You walked back to the tent. You were done.

Jimmy and his wife had come after all, and so had Nick. Dolan Connor was there too, Peterburden's one surviving friend. You saw Waverly making eyes at him as she lifted her place board to her face, taking a sip of tea and spilling. Or maybe it was whiskey. There were some open bottles on the table, and the guests were being loud now. Dolan didn't notice Waverly's attempts, his head was down, poor guy. No matter what mourning must become, it has to be truly rough to be one of the last survivors of your generation.

No one noticed you at first. You just stood there looking for a moment until Lucille screeched.

"Oh, he's back!"

Everyone looked up. They smiled at you. They applauded and hollered and pounded on the table.

"So are you going to take us to see them or what?" Lucille asked.

"I could use a new door, myself," Bet said, with as close to a grin as her frowning face allowed.

Nick handed you a drink, which you were grateful for, and you led the brigade across the field. It was slow going. A walker got abandoned on the way and Jimmy Downs carried poor Vernie on piggyback. She laughed so hard she peed, but "It didn't leak through!" she cried, lucky for Jimmy.

When they arrived at the first door everyone hushed for a moment. Someone whistled.

"I want to see them all," Jean said. "Every single one."

They strolled single file for a while, admiring the diversity of shape, size, grain, and knob. Ladies were into knobs. You said that out loud, because it was true, but Lucille and Bet got a real kick out of it. "I guess that was the problem wasn't it!" Emma put her arm around your waist and you moved to the back of the bunch. She hip checked you, a small punishment for abandoning her to host alone. You hip checked her back and it became a game. You smelled whiffs of Irish Spring and

Shalimar perfume from the women. You moved along taking in the night until the crowd stopped abruptly at a door somewhere in the middle of the line.

"Oh, this is just *amazing*," Sherri said. The others at the head of the group were agreeing and reaching out their hands to touch the wood. It was the first door you'd ever made. There was nothing fancy about the craftsmanship, but it was a gorgeous piece of flame maple. "Your first should be a beauty," Peterburden had said. You'd never trembled as badly as when you ripped into that block. But you refused to let yourself mess it up. You had taken breaks and put your tools down. Peterburden just handed you glasses of water. He understood.

Your guests understood too. It was a comfort. Lucille being Lucille said, "Well I can't help it anymore, I gotta walk through!" and turned the handle. You were too late with your protesting, she was through, and the others followed, breaking the line. You and Emma were the last ones in, and there was your big humiliating pile of sheets. You'd meant the line of doors to cover the mess. Hadn't expected entry. Everyone stared at the big sloppy hill and passed glances back and forth. Then Lucille stepped forward holding Sherri's hand and plopped herself down on the pile pulling Sherri down with her. Everyone laughed.

"Well I suppose I could use a rest," Sherri said, prim Sherri pinned in her purple suit, and everyone laughed harder. The two women stretched out their arms behind them and flapped and kicked their legs as they nestled in, miming the making of sheet angels. Lucile patted the sheets beside her. "Come on, " she said.

One by one, and two by two, the guests climbed and collapsed onto the sheets. Jimmy helped Vernie down. Waverly made sure she was next to Dolan. All the guests were laid out with heads on shoulders and arms behind heads, legs tangled and hands rested on hands. A word came to mind you couldn't remember the full meaning of. Alveolate. You and Emma got on last and it was surprisingly comfortable, soft and warm. Cavities, it meant. A couple of laughs rippled through the crowd. "I haven't been a part of a puppy pile in ages," Jean said. "It's nice."

They all eventually stopped talking. You had shut the door behind you, blocking the headlights from the truck, and you were glad you did. The stars were multitudinous. It seemed they would fall into your eyelashes if you weren't diligent with your depth perception. They made lattice work and lettuce patches, they swirled and blotted, and webbed and stitched, another record. A reflection, the aerial view. You were all fossils waiting to happen, fibers for the sky to rub down on, and that was fine. Someone sighed. A cool wrinkled arm lay beside yours. You were still as an eggshell. Quiet.

the lips the teeth the tip of the tongue

1. *The Have and the Want.* **Ongoing. Mixed Media. 4'9" x 10".**

In an auction there is always the have and the want. Baby Girl Bristol was a prodigy, truly, in the world of auctioneering. Her tongue trilled and twirled numbers like sparkler batons at a mere eight years old. She'd watched and watched and practiced in the tub. Her genius was unveiled quite to the surprise of her classmates and teacher in a casual episode of daily show and tell. Standing there kicking her ankle and fussing with her hair until she started and then it was the open-mouthed bewilderment of watching magic, meteor showers. Parents were alerted, scholarships secured, and she was shipped off to a school. Her instructors couldn't break the freakish habits she'd developed in the tub, though. She sang. All auctioneers sang, right, but Baby Girl Bristol *sang*. She clapped her hands and stomped her feet and danced, the numbers were melodies and the bidders were stuck in jolly good moods and so she peddled those heifers like no one before or since. Old seasoned professional auctioneers scratched their cowboy hats and rustled their beard hairs. Thirty and thirty and thirty I have do I have thirty-five thirty FIVE I have thirty I have thirty looking for looking for thirty five thank you ma'am thirty FIVE now I want forty forty now forty? So fast it sizzled. Snapped. Sold.

2. *Girl Descends*. 2013. Concrete and Rope. 5'6" x 15".

Baby Girl Bristol now had thirty-five. Years. She lived in Brooklyn and hadn't dusted off her lips in close to two of them. She had traveled the international circuits, sold thousands of farm animals, collectable action figures, and some art. Maybe that's what had changed her. Settled down in New York to be near the art.

She didn't tell her cynical friends that had taken years to make what she did so well. She was afraid to sound provincial. It was bad enough her hick accent still piped its bald head up sometimes. But Sotheby's had hired her for a special themed folk art event and a write up had wound up on page six. Bertrand saw, told them all. They rustled her hair and chuckled, cajoled her into demonstration. She got them up out of their seats at a crowded brunch spot. Even though she was being extra quiet, tables took notice and involved themselves. Her friends began to dance and clap and soon neighboring parties were spilling their mimosas. She gave in. Sold all of the restaurant's napkin holders, tables, chairs and carafes by the end and reduced a crowd of fifty to sweaty, foot stomping, numeral-hollering messes. They loved it.

She had a heck of a time convincing them that she was only playing and they couldn't keep the items they'd bid thousands of dollars on. Irony had been the fashion for so many years now and was always seeking out something new to make fun of, and love, and they found it in her. Bertrand and Mylo were all over it. A group show at their gallery was assembled over clinking sugared rims and a kickoff party would feature her as a centerpiece. They ordered a mechanical bull to rent and set up swings made of rope and hay bales around the space. Pies were baked and cowboy hats would be rocked. But BGB had a problem.

For years she had been sneaking private messages into her chants. Okay, from the beginning. When she was a wee lass of six now seven, she had six, does she hear seven, her parents were beginning talks about a looming divorce that had taken five years, now six, to complete. She needed a safe space to talk about her feelings but her parents were firm faced farmers, not a frown, not a smile, but a flat line. Keep working, keep close the mundane, because the mundane is solid and we, we are not. Neither were comfortable with tears or questions or observations, though at seven, now eight, eight, she had many rather astute ones. Instead of burdening her peers who seemed quite content to chew on erasers and stick yarn in their braces, or her teachers with their perfectly hair sprayed bouffants feeding Scantrons into grading machines, she took to integrating her unexpressed thoughts into her chants.

Auctioneers use filler words in their chants. They happen at hyper speed and sound like trills. Their purpose is to keep the chant at the pace of the bidding. Most use things like: *would you give me?, can I hear, thank you ma'am, right here, now we're at, I see you in the back, anywhere I can get it, I'm looking for, come on bidders now, say it, I have, I want,* and dot dot dot. Baby Girl, or properly, Janie, filled in her song with things like: *her eyes were red, Mom or Dad?, they're both nitwits, I'm scared, nobody can hear me, we're going to move, French kissing is gross, someone found the stupid letter, I can't breathe sometimes, if I died they would learn, anywhere is better than here, Say it, I have, I want,* and dot dot dot. So that the resulting auction might be saying something like: Get me out of here forty, hear me forty five, forty five, forty FIVE, the sonofabitch forty, my house was sold forty FIVE, in the back forty FIVE, not coming back fifty, fifty, fifty, I never wanna be fifty. Etcetera. But the audience only heard the numbers.

The habit had never been squashed. *Bullies should all die my best friend tried heroin they don't like me his eyes his eyes his eyes.* She actually felt incapable of conducting a proper auction entirely focused on the item in question. It bored her and it simply wasn't her art form. Her art form was secrets. When she didn't have any of her own, she would take to exposing the secrets of her audience. "She's cheating on you FIFTY FIFTY FIFTY it's obvious."

So she had learned to avoid being recorded. It wasn't a problem in the earlier days where it only took one family camcorder catastrophe to learn her lesson, but it had gotten harder and harder with cell phones and share-it-before-you-even-experience-it living. She had a contract she used—sometimes she was denied jobs because of it—but she couldn't risk someone slowing down the sound. Once a boy with Aspergers had gone into stitches at a comic book auction. He was the first person ever to decipher her filler words on his own and he found it absolutely hilarious. That's what he kept saying: "ABSOLUTELY HILARIOUS!" in between screeches. "YOU NEVER CALLED THE SCHMUCK!?" Hahahaha. "HILARIOUS!"

If video existed, surely someone would slow it because that's what people did to auctioneers. They tried to learn their tricks. So, no problem, contract says no audio or video, take it or leave it. But the gallery Bertrand and Mylo ran had an international internet community, people from the art world could attend opening nights virtually from Paris or Milan or Mozambique. They were recorded, streamed, archived and had a fair viewership, actually, because these boys knew how to throw a party right. There was always some kind of giant installation, street party, bizarre act of entertainment. Someone always went nude or swung from silks, marching bands led them hungry into sidewalk masses.

3. *Signs*. 2013. Reproduction and Ink. 8" x 10".

She'd given them her contract and they'd teased her. "So *professional!*" But they were no strangers to the often costly needs of eccentric artists. They read it over. Mylo said, Mylo, the sweet one, the gay one, the one with the square framed glasses, tufty black hair and smooshie lips, he said, "Everything is great Janie. Perfect. We'll just have to record it, obviously." And she had said, "Yes of course." ! Let me repeat: ! Never, ever, had Janie agreed to a recording. Never. Ever. She did not know why that passive utterance of agreement passed the captious grip of her teeth. Bertrand, the hot one, the straight one, the one with the chiseled cheekbones and slightly thinning hair had been staring at her, smiling. Dammit.

For weeks now she'd been planning sabotage. Imagining sneaking into the gallery in the middle of the night and dumping the cameras in buckets of water. Smearing Vaseline on the lenses. Stealing audio components. She had a key, she could do it. But they would suspect her. She'd brought it up three times now, "About the video thing..." They had given her Oh honeys and Come ons. She had claimed copyright on her style, she had said her profession depended on her being un-mimicable. "Welcome to this millennium, sweetheart. We open source, now." Open sorcery.

"Besides, no one in our crowd will be aspiring auctioneers," said Mylo.

They were wrong of course. You've got to love irony. How versatile a source it is for trendsetters—all is material and all at an arm's length.

The plan was this: Baby Girl was going to be a big girl. Chant like a champ, straight shooter, I have this, I want this, I see you in the back, do I hear...? No confessions of illicit affairs or unsavory feelings, no streams of consciousness, no finger pointing or ranting, just pure auction—what is for sale. What is for sale. She practiced and she practiced hard. It should have been easier. Conventional wisdom says that it's harder to trill with unpracticed phrasery. But BGB was so accustomed to merging her inner life and mind's eye with figures that separating the two proved tiresome. Not just tiresome. She felt like a stone. She wavered between feeling like a stone and bursting into tears over goat cheese crepes. While she hadn't been on the circuit in two years, she still allowed herself to sell a cow or two in the shower or while she mopped the floor. This self-censorship was rendering her a mess like everyone else. She was as bad as the townsfolk, no longer the composed hip urbanite she had cultivated herself to be, practically a man in her artful feigned emotionlessness. Hair styled, boots on, belt buckled, bag secured—no. Hair disheveled, makeup smeared, clothes an hour to pick out, friends alarmed.

4. *Mimosa/Mimesis*. 2013. Projection on Surface. Varied Dimensions.

She begged again, but Bertrand put his hand on hers and stroked her cheek. She was pancakes. His eyes fried her eggs into omelets. Name the breakfast she became in his company.

5. *Girl Gets Dressed*. 2013. Drapings and Body Casts. 5' 9" x 12"

The day came, as days do. Poor Baby Girl, poster child for good intentions, she was up early, practicing. Three and a half, four, four, FOUR, now help me out, four is what I'm looking for, yes four, yes four, I have three and a half help me with four, Ape on Bike—lovely in the living room, say four, Artist huge in Berlin, beat the crowd, thank you four, four and a half? Four and a half on Dad's credit card, four and a half he'll forgive you, Ape on Bike at a bargain ... Etcetera. Her lips like merry spokes she sang her speak and to an untrained ear it sounded like hummingbirds or a regularly serviced motorcycle engine. But to her it sounded dead. She understood the subtleties. Conducting a room was about going there, meeting people in their self-spaces and the only way out into them, was in, into her. They wouldn't hear the words but they would ride it anyway, ride where she took them. Sadness and joy are so close.

She never planned the confessions that became her filler words. She found out what was bothering her and what was beautiful to her by what came out. She worried that something quite big was bothering her. She worried that she had left the circuit so she wouldn't find out. She clenched her jaw and put braids in the sides of her wavy ashen hair. She got dressed in the costume B. and M. had picked for her. Gingham. A joke. She looked like a picnic and wished she was.

6. *Spin.* 2013. Video on loop.

She arrived at the space early to the hustle bustling of over-caffeinated artists installing their work. She saw the lighting people and the sound people setting up in the foyer where she would perform and she turned right back around. Her heart became eurhythmic. Sweet dreams were made of this. She slipped into a local dive. It was only three. Plenty of time to have a quick drink and shoot a game or two of pool. Opening was at six.

7. *There Were No Cameras.* 2013. Lenses. One Size Fits All.

And, well, let us get to the point, yes? What is coming down the line as sure as the thunder of the El with a loosed caboose. Two years we'll remember it has been for Miss Janie, and then Baby Girl has two bourbons.

She practiced on some dude who was trying to hit on her at the bar. It went well. She auctioned off the eight ball and the pool sticks and then the table. She only once entered her dream space and only, for some reason, to talk about rect-angles. Too many rectangles in New York City and fifty now fifty, hallways and elevators and fifty five and narrow rooms have fifty need fifty five and subway platforms and the pillars and the new compartments with the blue seats all rectangles rooms and rooms and rooms and buildings now sixty even roads fifty five now sixty.

Of course all Some Dude heard was her twirling tongue while he wondered what else she could do with it. She girled one last drink out of him and left the rectangle of the table. She got her rectangular credit card from the rectangular bar and left the rectangular room while he was in the lavatory (rect-angle). There were no cameras.

8. *The Silk Road #17: The Have and The Want*. Past-Present. Site Specific Performance.

And meanwhile back at the ranch the slender and the nar-row-hipped had assembled and were sipping. Janie was feeling loose. When she saw them all being intentionally and unin-tentionally awkward she felt a bubbly generosity. She plucked a champagne right out of an acquaintance's hand and smiled and walked off. Into the main gallery to get to know her art for the night, which in truth she should have done hours ago. She didn't worry. She knew these artists, all upstarts, one of them she even loved. The work chiaroscuroed nightmarish charac-ters holding misplaced symbolic objects in tiny, tiny hands. She made notes for her set-ups on her phone that she wouldn't carry. Never forget, she thought. She must have thought that.

All of this I know because there were cameras, of course, rolling. Digital holes filling digital hungers with bits of audio and visual echoes instantaneously assembling to tell more than the picture of a night. A reflection of the mismatched maps of a voice. Voices. See yourself there.

Let's get to the good part where you form your opinion.

Here is a transcription:

Picture it. She's walking up on stage with her braids and gingham, a little tipsy but in control of her faculties—innocent eyes, the kind with those lashes, facing a room of glitz and glitter. Circus freakdom meets nerd imitation meets shitkicker theme, or simple dark pants, refined style nodding to the night with bandanas tied to bags, hollers and serious faces not drunk enough yet. She takes the stage. Her genius is buzzing warmth into her vocal chords and her teeth are practically chattering to touch her tongue. She's excited. It's been too long. She lets a hillbilly hat tap of a touch of her accent into her mouth. At this point she probably knows already. She wants it. She's in heat for it. Her heart is pounding for the way the rhythms and the numbers let her down under and into herself, the one comfortable landscape, dreams snug in time signatures, figures, and crowds. She makes a valiant effort against the choo choo choo of her rattling heart and that light shining ahead, full steam. But when does fighting the heart ever work out? So, Baby Girl:

(Steps onto the stage. Clapping. She waits for silence.)

Friends. Romans. Brooklynmen. And women. Lend me your money. (Polite chuckles.) Actually … giveittome:

AND

I have an Ethan Night original, this is brand new folks we're starting at five on this one I need five to start us off that's

K, five K for Blood Moon Knockoff in Grey, I have five thank you I need fifty FIVE now (and already, already they are starting to move) I have five look at the shifting of light fifty five, a balloon about to burst that's potential, now five, and fifty five, potential in your living room fifty FIVE, picture it thank you fifty five, I want six, say six, come on and say six talented artist here I said bursting (and maybe it was this word that sent her) like on a highway and they said it was nerves, fifty five now SIX, hadn't seen him in too long shifting light and think of all the LAID you'll GET (she slowed it down enough for them to hear that part—the rest remember, sounds almost like one long rolled "r" interrupted only by prices) and thank you SIX, that got him, Six to the gentleman in the bowtie, elegant I have six, want sixty five, now six for sex, yes, can I hear sixty five, say it and that got him that I stood on the side of the interstate naked thank you sixty five we are cooking with grease now sixty five I want SEVEN, I'll get seven, my insides spewing out of my mouth and my ass in the road and I embarrassed him, SEVEN, sixty five come on y'all seven with the shit and the honking it wasn't nerves I was ten, SEVEN to the braless lady, thank you seven (people had begun to clap and Baby girl herself started stomping her feet) and SEVENTY FIVE now seven, looking for cover seventy FIVE, left when I was seven, I lie, it was younger, it was older, give me seventy five, it was years and the light didn't shift it bent seventy five, yes seventy FIVE to skinny jeans, thank you eight, now seventy five, then eight, seventy five, eight NOW, EIGHT now, I held on to a rock tight and closed my eyes for EIGHT shame, too fast to wipe up what came out I held onto a rock and the sky say seventy FIVE, come on EIGHT times we stopped the car, I said eight and

seventy five pieces of corn in the chunks of my gut but what
a regurgitation to talk about regurgitation, seventy five, look
at the shine of the fingernail on the hand of this man, his balloon and the air inside on your face and your dates thank you
EIGHT, Eighty five? I burst right in his face exploded daughter
how do you like it do you know eighty FIVE what you did to
her EIGHT years going once at EIGHT to the mustache, Eight,
always going going and the cars and you Eight our hearts going
twice this is Blood Moon Knockoff in Grey, say eighty FIVE
last chances are a bitch no one ever survives them I have eight
going (clap stomp clap sway) three times. And SOLD! ...to the
mustache.

(Whooooohooooooo!!!!   Heeeeeeehaaaaaaaaw!!!!!!   The
crowd claps like the roof falls.)

Next up I have "My Love Life" by Kathy McBride.

(One: Official Interlude number one. Should I remove the
numbers yet? The costs? Should I translate? Could the right
punctuation right this?)

(Two: Should I do them all? *My Love Life*, photo documentation of a performative marriage in which Baby Girl confesses
her feelings for Bertrand? *Heraclitus and the Birds*, painting
of an inside out face and a flock of cocks, a palimpsest over a
copy of the U.S. Constitution in which Baby Girl laments the
lighting of Facebook candles instead of real ones to remember
disasters instead of the ordinary? *Dick*, *Jane*, and *Puppy*, a trip-
tych from the chiaroscuro guy where average characters with
distorted foreheads each clutch objects in shrunken palms: an
egg, a spoon, and a severed duck head in which Baby Girl re-
members a dream she had about killer manatees that came
up onto the shore and ate people right off of their feet until

the jetties and the rock walls bore bloody ankle stumps as far as the eye could see? The manatees had to be burned out. It singed the skin of those trapped with them but, oh, the return to the ocean. Should I go on? Should I do them all?)

(Three: Because the presence in the room that night, the bodies in hum guzzling electricity, and cracked open heart chords snap clapping knee slaps and sweat smiling, bodies in love with other strange bodies without even telling the brains they belonged to, leaving them out of it, the joy only fist pumped by the underscore of the sadness of our Baby Girl— the money aflow—the he*art* changing hands. This was the important part. Have you formed your own opinion?)

(Four: But whatever happened to Baby Girl? We know the tapes were, in fact, slowed, and that every wrinkle on the curves of her soul stood buck naked and waving in the rainclouds. And not just her soul, but her judgments, because if you think she didn't make some fun of those hipsters well, come on. And not just her judgments but her fears, the worst thing, right, I mean the worst thing to become a spinning mannequin in a storefront window. In the curmudgeonly art world no less. But this is the thing: people ate it up. Once and awhile the video still pops up on a blog, or the audio on a streaming public radio program in the middle of the night, fast to slow, fast to slow, but never without popping into oblivion as fast as it popped into view. In some young counter culture circles she's now a sort of mythical heroine, an urban legend that gets passed with the bowl now and then, because people rather enjoy having their flaws pointed out as it turns out, and they rather enjoy demonstrations of genius, even quirky ones made of the lips the teeth the tip of the tongue, and they especially eat up a mystery. Some say she wound up in Detroit, some say Berlin or L.A. Some say she went back to heifers. Certainly some of the interested audio geeks had tried to find her because unclaimed fame is hard to swallow. Certainly I'm not saying whether they're saying or who is, and how much.

What did Janie actually do when she was done that night?

She walked out onto a wet street and smelled the rock of the city she hugged herself and became her secret.)

arrivederci

The two shared a monster. The monster shared the two. Duplicates of the monster, which were still the monster, lived in each of the two, in their sternums. Usually. The two were named Bud and Blue. The monster was named Arrivederci. It named itself when Bud and Blue were taking an Italian cooking class and the chef would call this word out to the couple as they walked out of the glass doors on oaky evenings. The word mixed with full bellies and cool air would create a rivulet the monster enjoyed in the breastplates of his homes. He wanted Bud and Blue to call to him and slide him a rivulet, or at least a bowl of gnocchi, but they never did. Bud and Blue wanted Arrivederci to go.

Most of the time they forgot their monster was even there, but sometimes he would become active. He was like a gymnast in these periods.

"Do you feel that?" Bud would ask Blue, who would look down and wipe her hair out of her eye.

"Like a swollen ox rolling?"

"Yes or a prick of steel wool wrapped in a wave."

"Yes or an envelope of explosive powder sealed with a kiss from a dead witch."

"Yes or a walk down an aisle of talcum powder layered over broken glass."

The two sat, sullen.

A stick, a horse jaw, a rancid punch, they went on. A bone thick bruise.

Arrivederci was only stretching his muscles. He was only lifting his legs, pressing his palms, even the handstands and somersaults were innocent. He liked to play the mirror game with the other side of himself, across the way, in the other gut. He would create emotional renditions of his feelings in large gestures that he would copy back to himself in sync. He could hear them complain, but he had no alternative, cooped up as he was in tissue without so much as a rivulet. Sometimes he wondered if his hosts even knew his name. Sometimes he wrote lists to fill the loneliness his homes inspired in him. He listed the words trapped in Bud and Blue, the ones that would float down in their blood. He compared the lists and tried to understand the truth about love.

Bud—stingy, stuffed, blanket, toast, archbishop, sorry, boobs.

Blue—twist, archipelago, cake, alabaster, spaghetti, Istanbul, microphone.

He found a similarity sometimes, like arch, and chanted the word to them, arch arch arch! He wanted them to understand the mirror game in them, but he only cramped their individuality.

Sometimes he got angry with them and would exact revenge by stealing a secret word from Blue and whispering it into Bud's blood. Blue, forgetting that they shared a monster would be beside herself when Bud looked into her eyes and knew the words she'd hid. That she had decided to go to Istanbul for a month without him, after all. That she was mad he didn't bake a cake for her birthday. She, too, could see how terribly sorry he was for coveting other women's boobs. Transparency is an uncomfortable quality and Arrivederci could see through it all.

When Arrivederci was pleased with his homes he sang sweet words into the blood of them, moon, river, rock-type words. Cup, he thundered, spoon. Puddle gloss, he whispered into their lungs. Underwood, libretto, paper boat. Bud and Blue would feel young again and connected by shared air, as if there were no such thing as Arrivederci, who in these moments was content to hum through the strings of his selves, invisible.

But when their monster rumbled and roared and push-upped! The two would tear at their hair and scream. We must hatch a plan they'd say, but Arrivederci smashed each egglet of a blueprint of a plan. The monster dismantled words when he was scrambled and felt his homes to be in jeopardy. The wrong words like leave would float up, or worse, none.

One egglet he didn't smash, though, couldn't. After the fighting Blue and Bud would sometimes melt into a froth of oohs and ahs and Arrivederci would close his ears and try to take a nap. Out of the froth of one of their ahs, Blue became pregnant. The word pregnant sang in their blood like the pleasant cramp of goodbye laced with thousands of handkerchiefs waving hello. At first Arrivederci plucked at the egglet. Sniffed it. Folded his arms. It was a boring companion. Arrivederci didn't like it. But then it grew a small tail and he couldn't help but take a liking to this veiny little tadpole beside him. He decided he would tell the changing egg with the tail hundreds of stories as it grew. He decided to tell the changing egg with the tail the one about the barber frowning, and the marionette winking, and the hen haggling. He wrote a list of important story subjects, and elaborated in evenings when Bud and Blue fell fast asleep.

For example:

Story Subjects—animal love, love, love, putrid people, fish tanks, sanguine dreams, love, delicate china, stupidity, apologies, barstool legs, fame, dilettantes.

Elaboration—There once was a Pekinese dog and a parakeet. They lived in a fancy old mansion, but were terribly bored because they were owned by ~~putrid people~~. The Putrid People completely forgot about them until guests came, at which time they would stretch out their arms as if saying "Tada!" and the guests would stare as the animals licked themselves, uncomfortable in the sudden glow. In the absence of ~~love~~, the dog and the parakeet grew to ~~love~~ one another. The dog would rest her head under the parakeet's gilded cage while the parakeet sang. He would blink his eyes rapidly so no one could catch him crying. The parakeet pretended she could only shriek in front of the putrid. For the dog alone she saved her beautiful notes."

Arrivederci paused the storytelling to swallow his spit and make sure the fetus was listening. The tadpole had recently lost its tail. It seemed to happen quite suddenly. Fingers and toes had pushed themselves out of its blood sacks and now Arrivederci was growing a real and annoying fondness for his tiny roommate. It looked like a monster! It had a giant angry looking head protruding over its unseeing eyes. It gave Arrivederci a rivulet just looking at this fetus, although he couldn't fully tell if the little beast was listening. It seemed so, so he went on with it.

"One day the Putrid People took the parakeet from its cage, shaking their heads, and walked right out the door. The dog was beside himself. Where were they taking his best friend? He searched the house for another friend to confide his terror to. Room after room was empty of life, but then the dog remembered the ~~fish tank~~ in the foyer and bounded to the front of the house. He stared up wide-eyed at the tank.

The fish wouldn't sing to him. They were big and yellow and striped and dumb. But he could hear one thing from them. It was less of a song and more of a glug. They sang-glugged, *Get me out of here.*

The dog wanted to make up for not rescuing the parakeet from the Putrid People so he tried to make this fish wish come true. He leapt at the fish tank with all of his might and knocked it down shattering.

The fish sang a different thing writhing on the floor. He felt sorry then and tried to lick life into their gills. They couldn't get oxygen from canine saliva though, so they began to die. The dog ate them to get it over with quicker. And because of their tantalizing smell. The dog was embarrassed that they were delicious.

When the Putrid People came home they had the parakeet in tow. She had just needed a check up at a horrible place called Vet. The dog was so happy the parakeet was back that he completely forgot what he had done. He leapt up on the Putrid People's legs in gratitude. But they didn't like that one bit, and further they could see the fish tank mess all around their feet. They thought the dog was a Big Problem. They whipped him and then took him to a kennel where no one sang, and the dogs were all miserable."

Animals don't understand about people's monsters, Arrivederci thought. He added "people's monsters" to his list before continuing his elaboration for the squinting fetus.

Ahem.

"The parakeet had no friends and spent her days molting, though at night when she slept she had ~~sanguine dreams~~ of her old dog friend. She pictured him cavorting on ~~barstools~~ with gazillions of parakeets, saving their best notes for him.

The Putrid People's guests one day noticed that the parakeet was molting. The Putrid People distracted the guests with paintings and wood grain, but when the guests left, the Putrid People did something they'd never done. They were putrid, but they did feel bad about the dog, and felt that upright citizens shouldn't have such unfortunate pets. For the first time in years, they questioned themselves. So they opened the tiny lock on the cage door to let the parakeet stretch her wings a bit in the grand old house.

The parakeet wasted not a minute. She knew what the Putrid People valued and went straight for the ~~delicate china~~ they had on display. She flew into that delicate china with all her might, hoping to be sent away to wherever her dog friend had gone. She broke the heirlooms to pieces, pleased with the firm punch of her own beak and the muscle in her wing.

The Putrid People ran around the house screaming. The bird wanted them to capture her, but even with her help they couldn't grasp such a swift and delicate thing. They opened a window, just wanting the wreckage to stop, because now the parakeet was poking holes in prized paintings. The parakeet wanted to see her dog friend with all of her might, but the call of the fresh wind when the window opened intoxicated her. She could think nothing but drink. She wobbled on the proverbial ~~barstool~~, with the proverbial short ~~leg~~. She couldn't take it. The air sucked her right out of the house, and her first free flight was a nectar so exquisite, she forgot all about her friend in the high of heights so high."

But not forever, Arrivederci explained. The fetus was grimacing. Arrivederci grimaced right back. He could hear Bud and Blue waking up, coughing and cursing for coffee, so he paused as he always did during days. He had to resume his daily job of stretching and begging for rivulets. For some reason the presence of the fetus had made him even more diligent in his work. He was barely sleeping. He had committed to a workout regimen and was growing strong muscles in both of his selves. Bud and Blue screamed their heads off a lot of the time, though the fetus seemed to have almost as much power over the two as Arrivederci did. They collapsed in puddles of soft voiced sighs almost as much as they hooted and hollered at each other. They would send down rivulets all right! But the rivulets never had Arrivederci's name on them. This was disconcerting to Arrivederci, especially because he had to admit that the fetus was having a similar effect on him. One day his jealousy got the best of him, though, and he kicked the fetus. The fetus kicked right back. Blue made a sound like, "Oh." This was the beginning of the kicking game, which they played and played. The fetus slyly won Arrivederci over in this way.

One day Bud and Blue had a new word in their blood. It was a word Arrivederci knew, but it was the way they said it that made it fall into his fists and vibrate. The word was "boy". Boy, boy, boy, they both chanted. It was uncomfortable for the monster. He had seen the penis, of course. He'd seen it before they squirted jelly on Blue's belly and rubbed a wand on her and she shouted with glee. But he had been avoiding it. The little penis growing there caused Arrivederci's forehead to wrinkle exceedingly. He didn't know what to do about his shifting predicament. For days he ceased his workout regimen. He stopped storying. He dropped his head in his hands in both of the sternums and stared at the penis as if challenging it. Herman kicked him right in the face.

"Herman!" Arrivederci yelled. "Herman, Herman, Herman!" It was Arrivederci's self in Bud's sternum that yelled the loudest.

The standoff between Arrivederci and the penis ended with the name. The monster was so happy with both his selves for coming up with the perfect name, a task that had befuddled the two. Once he sang it into the blood of Bud and Blue, it was official. But now the rivulets that came down not only didn't have Arrivederci's name on them, they had Herman's name. He could no longer pretend that every fifth one was really for him and mistakenly sent to the fetus.

Luckily his muscles had grown strong. It felt more important than ever to resume his storytelling now that a plan was growing in him like an egg.

So he did: His voice took on gravity:

"After swooping and diving and perching, and diving again, after she scoped the town and the lakes and streams, ate six worms and dodged a cat, the parakeet remembered what she was supposed to be doing and gulped. She resolved to begin a search.

She asked far and wide if anyone had seen a dog that weighs seventy pounds and blinks a lot. She asked a squirrel who shrugged, among other things. She asked a deer who dodged, among other things. She asked a rat who ran, among other things. Nothing. She asked so many animals that the dog became ~~famous~~.

One day she saw a great mastiff with crust in his eyes being walked on a leash. She recognized the people yelling at the dog (who was trying to obey but confused by the shouting). They were Putrid People. Not *her* Putrid People. But perhaps the world was filled with putridity. She flew up to the mastiff's ear to the chagrin of the Putrid and sang a message she hoped would help him. She then told the mastiff her story while the people batted at her and spun and squawked. If you ever see him, please, she begged.

The days passed slowly, but pass they did. Once, the dog, lying in his kennel listening to the others snore thought he heard the parakeet's soft song in the night. He was right. She'd been flying overhead, searching. He wept and wept at the sound, and one of the other dogs nodded his head at one of the other other dogs.

The crying dog! They all began to yap.

Because he had become famous across the land, all of the dogs perked up. They wagged their tails and scratched at their cages. One among them had spoken to the parakeet, though.

The great old Mastiff with crust in his eyes made his way to the edge of his cage. Something in his eyes made all the dogs sit as if it were treat time. He began to tell the full story series of The Parakeet's Search. The Searching Bird and the Shrugging Squirrel, the Searching Bird and the Dodging Deer, the Searching Bird and the Running Rat."

But those are other stories, Arrivederci interrupted himself, for another day, he told the egglet. He made a note on his to-do list to tell the tinier tales inside the tale and then wondered if there were then more tales inside of those, and what if he himself was in a larger tale, and that tale was in a still-larger tale? But then the word tale lost its meaning and the world felt too enormous and he felt dizzy. He put away his notes for the night because the sun was rising the phlegm up out of his homes.

Arrivederci thought he would kick start the day with a few rounds of jumping jacks, but Blue had woken up with a loud hankering for chocolate cake. Arrivederci loved the word "cake" so he perked up. When Bud brought the plate to Blue the conversation devolved into something called "birth plan" and Arrivederci strained his ears. Birth Plan had been coming up lately. Usually when Birth Plan came up, it was high time for a back flip or two, but the weight of their voices was different so Arrivederci remained still. The words that floated down were pretty boring. Home, hospital, drugs. Some were nice like water and music. But what struck Arrivederci was the phrase uttered by Blue: "We have to decide now, Bud. We only have three months."

Three months! Arrivederci did a sequence of nervous squats. A monster should know these things, he scolded himself. A monster shouldn't get so lost in time all the time! While Bud and Blue commenced fighting about preventing a thing called C-section, Arrivederci shaped himself into warrior pose. He realized two things, one in each of his extending selves. 1. He would never have time to tell all of the stories, not even all of the stories inside of one single story. 2. He had to try.

That night, after Bud and Blue had made their Birth Plan, which included the excellent word "tub", Arrivederci had his notebook ready before they even fell asleep. He began with the Searching Bird and the Shrugging Squirrel, a story about how food and riches are great unless you let them twist your heart into a tiny numb acorn.

Baby Herman had grown eyebrows and used them to eye Arrivederci suspiciously. The monster would not be distracted by infantile skepticism, however. When he got to the part about the squirrel taunting the parakeet and found another story hidden in there, about the squirrel's siblings torturing her to compete for their parent's affection, he let himself slide into it. Inside of that was a story about the squirrel's parents, and inside of that was one about her grandparents, and on and on all the way back to the Epic Battle of One Winter, the tale where all of the animals grew limbs to match their skills after a Dark Wizard nearly took them all out in the forms of each other. The path to that story was riddled with side stories about friends and trees and frozen lakes. It was tough work ignoring them, but it was all about focus Arrivederci told himself.

In the morning he was so exhausted he could only half-heartedly stretch. Acting out seventeen renditions of nested tales for a pre-lingual mind is terribly tiring. "You try it!" Arrivederci said angrily to an imagined audience.

The nights continued like this—frantic and full. Herman was looking handsome by the end of the seventy-three iterations of the stories stuffed in the Searching Bird and the Dodging Deer. The baby's skin had thickened and smoothed while Arrivederci sent him words like "spots" and "fear" and enacted deadlocked horns and trembling legs and all manners of beastly bodies hiding in labyrinthine forests. Herman had been flipping around for a while but now seemed to have gotten comfortable with his head pointing down.

The nights grew weirder and weirder as Arrivederci explored the innards of the Searching Bird and the Running Rat. By now he was so adept at the Trend that he had begun breaking it apart. He was finding horrific and complicated humanity inside of a simple stare down between a rat and an exterminator! He was unable, sometimes, to express it in animal terms, and had resorted to human ones, philosophical treatises, even cracking open the words themselves and experimenting with the implications of their order. He had resorted to poetry.

He'd noticed the Trend one hundred and four stories ago. Still he had been fascinated by it for some time and had a love for it even now. It went like this: in every single story one element thwarted another. Conflicts of battle and blood, spillage, metaphoric or real, in the words and under. Thwart thwart thwart went the tales and Arrivederci had had the gall to wonder why? What more? But not the gall to know the answer! He was sure he would never finish the telling in time for the Birth Plan. The Birth Plan was thwarting him!

Baby Herman was groaning. Not from his mouth, but from within.

By day all of Arrivederci's nervous energy was upsetting Blue. "Hot" she said, over and over, "pissed". He wasn't trying to upset her, even though there was no chance of a rivulet these days. He just wanted Herman to be prepared. It's all anyone wants, he thought sadly.

He knew now that even with all of his muscles and lists, he was insufficient. Worse, his beloved words were.

The bird/rat business had left poetry behind and turned into a harsh sound massage by the end. "Ah ah ah. Oh/oh and a bite/a/bang ah." He decided to have mercy on himself and scrap it. Baby Herman was blinking at him. The Birth Plan was any day now.

He had to return to the larger story. He hoped he would find something more there.

It took him a minute to remember where he had left off. The kennel returned to him, though. The domesticated and caged, scratching to get close to something they perceived as bigger than themselves.

Arrivederci shook his head and took on the voice of the Mastiff while Blue's sternum and Herman's feet pressed against his lungs.

This is it now:

"I spoke to her," the Mastiff said to the dog. The parakeet, he meant. She asked me if I ever met you to tell you…she's so sorry.

So very sorry, the Mastiff repeated, lowering his head.

The dog didn't understand.

The air was too strong. She wanted to be here with you, the bird, but the air was too strong."

Arrivederci thought for a moment about how the dog would feel hearing something like this. Then Arrivederci himself felt it.

"She's free?" The dog asked, and upon the drool drenched nod of the Mastiff before him—the dog began to leap with joy.

The parakeet was free and had not forgotten him.

Arrivederci paused here for effect. He had lightened his own mood with the truth of how beautiful things sometimes escape.

"And do you know what happened?" He asked Herman.

"Well it's true that the dog lived out the rest of his days happy, and cheered up his bunkmates as well, who all admired him because he was the most famous dog they'd ever met. They played pool and poker and told stories. The kennel workers were less putrid then their original people—some were even ~~dilettante~~ artists—and the canines carved out a life for themselves, however small. Sometimes at night the dog dreamed of sweet songs under gilded cages. On those nights what was dream and what was real blended sweetly enough to fill a sky."

Herman was fast asleep. The monster patted himself on the back. He felt a little cheap. But in a good way. Plus he had a new plan. It would never work for him the way it did for the parakeet, because he was a monster. Doomed to expand. But at least it was a move toward something. Instead of just away from a thwart.

Quietly, Arrivederci whispered as many more stories as he could, so Blue and Bud couldn't hear, and so that the stories would blend into dreams like they did in the stories, but Herman had grown so fat with tales and food and he pushed down hard against Arrividerci. It made the kicking seem like raindrops by comparison. He pushed and pushed and it got tight, so tight in both of the sternums. Even Bud's.

The baby couldn't care about dogs and birds forever, he had to grow. Arrivederci was moved by his strength. He knew what was coming and knew Herman would need it.

Birth Plan had arrived. It was time for Blue to get the baby out. All of the falling words said fuck and the rumble was like nothing kickboxing Arrivederci could ever create. A tempest of fluid and press beset him, squished into the tiniest corner, face smashed against Blue's costal cartilage, feet curled and bent into a vertebrum. He knew he had to break off a part of himself, like Blue was doing, like Bud was doing, like even the little baby called Herman was doing. It would hurt but he would third himself, send a triplicate out with the child, and would sing across the strings to whole himself later. If he made it.

Together, he and Blue screamed. A monster dividing is a sacred but brittle act. Wiped in mucas and muck, raw as it is, the pain and splendor cannot be summed up with rolling oxen or poisons. A monster dividing is how the earth got here. A split as deep as stars inverting. The screams of the whole family crescendoed, bending the air of the room into an awful shimmer.

After he had gathered his selves and was splitting for good, Blue called to him. "Arrivederci!" She yelled, her voice like swallowed thunder, but it was too late. His new third had half swum down Herman's mouth, far from the rivulet with his name on it, readying himself for his next life-long goodbye.

"Do you feel that?" Blue asked Bud, when the room returned to calm. They were staring at the soft hairs upon little Herman's head while he took his first glimpses of the world.

"Like rosettes of sweet cream ice, enough to fill a sea?"

"Yes, or a floating picnic in a painting of clouds?"

"Yes, or a bar of ballerinas cuddling chinchillas."

"Yes, or a hammock of pillows strung from the sky."

The two sat, awestruck.

"A gathering wave, a silken kiss, a sign at the airport," they went on. "A life long dream."

Arrivederci rested quietly in Herman where the falling blood words were simpler for now. Mom, Dad, food. Bud and Blue could hardly feel Arrivederci at all until some mornings when Herman would cry with the fervor of fever and sleep had been scarce. Then the whole family would mirror the horror film in each other while Arrivederci stretched his legs in glee.

He didn't worry as much about his muscles growing flabby these days. His nights were spent betraying the secrets of Bud and Blue to their son, but not the secrets of the boy, which were too complex as wordless as they were. He dreaded the day when his new home became crowded and the stories were forgotten and the lists began. For now he was savoring his time teaching the child the words of his parent's story. But that's another story.

"Bye bye!" Herman learned to say one day, and the parents clapped with joy. He's so smart, they beamed. And they were right. He opened and closed and opened his hand.

shush

Oh, it was scary, my ride on the concrete boat. There is such a thing as a concrete boat, you know. Don't want you to go down the wrong stream. We started gently down the stream, in fact. That's exactly what we did.

Things were going well, the sun was sparkling the tree leaves, the water lapped and licked. We were high up. We should have understood. On the drive, the layered view of patchy hills and rock faces and the puffy cloud proximity pulled us far from ground. But the river rocked us gently and the boat felt so sturdy, concrete and all.

Then it narrowed—first it narrowed, the river, into a stream. It sloped downward and we picked up speed. We giggled at first. We had lifejackets; we had a heavy boat beneath our flip-flops. It had been planned and there were guides. Soon, though, the slope dove nearly vertical, leveled and dropped again. Bloop bloop the stomachs went like water, the fish inside water, the birds above water. The hands gripped the shoulders. The eyes looked at the other eyes to compare wideness. A man's hat flew off. Blurs of green leaves like needles bulleted by and wayward branches spit, flung like the lassos of drunken heroes. The boat began going so fast that it was coming up off of the track of the stream, lifting at shifty intervals. You might call the river a waterfall now, so steep its pour, but still hugged by banks on its sides. You take comfort in the presence of banks, let me tell you, when your concrete boat is nose down.

We hit a hard bump and then sailed. "Clear in the air." It looked as if we might go right off of the mountain but the boat galumphed back onto the water and took a sharp turn with the course of the flow. I child-hoped for a moment that this was a man-made ride, silly hopes. Men are good about planning for death, better than pure nature is. By now death was expected. We'd done our screams and gone quiet, holding hands and grinding teeth. I surrendered to snatching some last beauties. I gulped air and pretended to be a bird or a leaf, some high thing with little density. I looked down the sides of the boat dizzy at the sight of rocks and water so snug and clingy below. I felt suddenly sorry for those low things I was, depending on each other and gravity. There was a seatbelt, though, so the ways in which I was air born were also communal. I was only one of a crowd strapped to a boat in the air, not me, a boat, and I couldn't be lost to the wind alone, the wind I inhaled with greed. I gulped air and was air. I was in, I was out.

Then a surprising thing happened, which is that we didn't die. We splashed down hard into a lake part of the river. We plunged under the water with the concrete and it hurt our bottoms, but nonetheless we emerged bobbing in a wider body. Our noses and ears had filled with rushing. Our lungs had emptied into bubbles. Gasps released our clenched and aching diaphragms, while our stunned bodies dripped and shook to the roar and ring. After the coughing exclamations, there was murmuring, but no one was the first to speak. The water made lake sounds once we got away from the falling river, quiet rolls, quiet weight, push and tug. Less sun was what I noticed—but bits of it still shined, pocketed shimmer balls like cupped hands holding fools gold through the trees, plussing glimmers on points and swells, piecing water. Silhouetted light will shatter into zillions of lines if you move even an eyelash. I like that.

The next thing I noticed, which should have been the first, is that we were approaching a colony of forty or fifty flamingos. They swam like ducks, kissing and licking feathers, biting themselves and each other, soft beaked. A flamboyance of pink necks, the letter "S" multiplied, they were gliding and peering with calm black eyes. Together the mass looked like a healthy lung, we, the inhalation. The quiet was slowly becoming quiet enough to hear submerged bird feet paddle. Little drops falling from wings were penny wishing, skipped rock tinkling. The concrete boat flowed into the flock. Most of the flurry watched us serenely, as if they knew some protected secret to which we'd lost the password. Some were kind enough to look away. As we floated closer they nipped our empty hands and hair. Such smiles broke with sighs. We slowed and shared a sunspot, small opened locket pearled with warmth and ease gone pink, gone water birded, gone boat.

It took a long time to work our voices again. When we finally did, we talked about other things.

acknowledgments

"Call Me Silk" is forthcoming from *Western Humanities Review*. "Free Baby" was recognized with an award from the National Society of Arts and Letters and was first seen in *Corium Magazine*. "The Lips the Teeth the Tip of the Tongue" appeared in the *Indiana Review*, "The Best Deal" in the *Slash Pine 2011 Poetry Festival Anthology*, and "Holy Property" in Tuscaloosa Writes This. "Corner" and "Our Acts Together" appear in *NANO Fiction* and the *Atlas Review*, respectively. "Songbun Song" is up at *Joyland*, "All She Had" at *Hobart*, and "Not the Problem" at *[PANK]*, respectively. I'm grateful to all of the people behind these publications, and editors Emily Schultz, Patti White, Brian Oliu, Brandi Wells, Joe Mayers, Trevor Mackesey, Peter Kispert, Britt Ashley, Natalie Eilbert, Dolan Morgan, Lauren Becker, and Kirby Johnson.

I love FC2. All of you. Thank you for making me a better

reader and writer and then inviting me into your formidable, miraculous tribe. Special thanks to Matt Roberson for choosing my book for the Sukenick and being gracious when my response was, "I think I might crash my car." Dan Waterman, Vanessa Rusch, JD Wilson, Kristi Henson, Courtney Blanchard, and Gail Aronson at the University of Alabama Press, you are patient saints of literature. Lance Olsen, you warm my heart and brain alike. Double special thanks and low bow to Ronald Sukenick.

One day maybe I will have a coolly brief acknowledgments page full of grace, but today is not that day. Thank you for your patience as I try to begin to thank the deserving hordes of beauties: the University of Alabama MFA Class of 2013, (also 2012, 2014, +); special shout to my band of dazzlers: Pink Stealth—featuring the stellar writers of hit songs Dara Ewing, Tessa Fontaine, Betsy Seymour, and Ashley Gorham; plus swings Rachel Adams, Jenny Gropp, Annie Agnone; and superstar readers and friends, Lisa Tallin, Danilo John Thomas, Farren Stanley. Really to the whole town of Tuscaloosa circa 2011, I hat tip with my whole hat. While on groups, my chin nods ever to the good people of Epic Theatre Ensemble. Fease. Teachers. Mr. Barnacle, Mr. Bruce, Malidoma Somé, Michael Martone, Suzanne Trauth, Wendy Rawlings, Joel Brouwer, Kellie Wells, Robin Behn, Joe Russo, Jim Nicosia, Sarah Barry. More teachers. My aunts. There are so many writers I love and some have also extended a hand to me, especially the wonderful Peter Markus, Joyelle McSweeney, and Alissa Nutting. Also Lydia Millet, the vivid! Roxane Gay, Kate Bernheimer, George Saunders, Aimee Bender, and torchbearer Luke B. Goebel have been so inspiring and kind. Lily Hoang, Noy Holland, and

Sabrina Orah Mark gave such helpful feedback on zygotes of these stories. My soul twin Aimee Senopole and recess partner Vy Duong, you are everything. Sebastian Masuelli, what shall I compare thee to? The loves Rebekka Johnson, BJ Gallagher, Rhea Ramey, Matt Donnelly, Jim Festante, Hope Thomas, Danny Manley, Katie Renn, Ashley Chambers, Anna Maron, clearest eyes. Big love to Randy Ford, are we there yet? Carolyn Richardson, my mommy salami, and Justin, Jaimie, Jennifer, Jonathon, and Jeremy, you are my hearts. Thanks to Sandi Shapiro and her J-clan too—John, Josh, Jordan, and especially Joseph...always. Thank you for loving some of these stories when they were babies. I wish you were here to see more black words breathe. My lifetime won't be enough to thank my extraordinary grandmother, Genevieve B. Richardson, and her grandmother before her. I hope to be always acknowledging you all, named and unnamed, in real time with my life. Thank you, thank you, on and on.